Dirty Bertie

TRiCKS AND KiCKS

DAVID ROBERTS WRITTEN BY ALAN MACDONALD

LITTLE TiGER

LONDON

Dirty Bertie

Collect all the
Dirty Bertie books!

Contents

STRIPES PUBLISHING LIMITED
An imprint of the Little Tiger Group
1 Coda Studios, 189 Munster Road,
London SW6 6AW

Imported into the EEA by Penguin Random House Ireland,
Morrison Chambers, 32 Nassau Street, Dublin D02 YH68

A paperback original
First published in Great Britain in 2021

Characters created by David Roberts
Text copyright © Alan MacDonald

ISBN: 978-1-78895-322-1

MIX
Paper from
responsible sources
FSC® C171272

The Forest Stewardship Council® (FSC®) is a global, not-for-profit organization dedicated to the
promotion of responsible forest management worldwide. FSC® defines standards based on agreed
principles for responsible forest stewardship that are supported by environmental, social, and
economic stakeholders. To learn more, visit www.fsc.org

10 9 8 7 6 5 4 3 2

Dirty Bertie

MASCOT!

For Bertie, for all the years of fun and laughs
~ D R and A M

Contents

MASCOT!

CHAPTER 1

Mum came into the kitchen carrying the post.

"Oh, Bertie, you've got a letter," she said.

Bertie hardly ever got any post apart from at birthdays and Christmas. He tore open the envelope.

"Wow!" he cried. "They want me to be a mascot!"

"That's nice," said Mum. "You've got jam on your face."

"A mascot for the school team?" asked Dad.

"No, for Rovers," replied Bertie. He read out the letter…

You're invited to be Rovers' match day mascot for the game against Mudchester City…

"Who's Rovers?" yawned Suzy.

"Pudsley Rovers!" said Dad. "Our local team – they're in Division One!"

"But why choose Bertie as their mascot?" asked Mum.

Bertie didn't have a clue. Then he remembered – months ago he'd put his name down for something to do with football. Darren had done it, too – he'd been wildly excited about the chance of being picked.

"I think I entered a competition," said Bertie. "Anyway, what's a mascot?"

"It's a huge honour," explained Dad. "Every team has a lucky mascot. You run out with the players and line up before kick-off."

Dirty Bertie

This didn't sound that exciting to
Bertie. He had to line up before school
every day.

"Do I kick the ball?" he asked.

"No! You're not *playing!*" said Dad.

"Do I blow the whistle then?"

"That's the referee's job," said Dad.

"Well, *what do I do?*" Bertie wanted
to know.

"I've told you, you cheer your team
on and bring them luck," said Dad.
"You'll probably meet Larry Lion."

"There's a *LION?*" said Bertie.

That would certainly make the game
more exciting. The players would have
to run for their lives!

"It's not a *real* lion," said Dad. "Rovers'
team mascot is Larry Lion. It's a man
dressed up in a lion costume."

Bertie frowned. "But I thought *I* was the mascot?"

"You're the *junior match day mascot*, which is different each time," Dad explained. "Larry Lion is the *team mascot* — he's there for every game."

Bertie thought it all sounded a bit complicated.

"Why can't I be the lion?" he asked.

Dirty Bertie

"Sorry, I don't think that's what they want," said Dad.

"They might," said Bertie. "The letter doesn't say I *can't* be the lion. Anyway, they haven't heard me roar yet. ROARRRRR!"

Mum and Dad covered their ears. They hoped Bertie wasn't going to get too carried away.

CHAPTER 2

Bertie couldn't wait to tell his friends on Monday morning.

"Guess what," he said, on the way to school. "I'm going to be a mascot!"

"You?" said Eugene. "What for?"

"For Rovers," answered Bertie. "Dad says they're really famous."

"I know who they are," said Darren.

Dirty Bertie

"My dad takes me to all the home games. But who says you're the mascot?"

"I got a letter on Saturday," said Bertie. "It must have been that competition we entered."

Darren's mouth fell open. "That's so unfair! You only entered because I did. You don't know anything about football!"

"I *do*! I played for the school team,"
argued Bertie.

"Only once, because no one else
would go in goal," said Darren.

"Anyway, they picked me," said Bertie.
"I've got to lead the teams out for the
kick-up."

"The kick-*off*," said Darren.

"But that's not the best bit," Bertie
beamed. "I'm going to dress up as a lion!"

"What?" said Eugene.

"You don't mean Larry Lion?" gasped
Darren. "They want you to be *Larry
Lion*?"

"That's right," said Bertie. "There are
two mascots but I'm definitely going to
be the lion one."

Darren and Eugene could hardly
believe it. Not only was Bertie going

to be a mascot – he got to wear a lion costume.

"Larry Lion is a legend," said Darren. "He gets the crowd laughing and cheering. He can even juggle a football!"

Bertie hoped they didn't want him to juggle. But he was good at making his friends laugh so he'd just have to stick to that.

"Well, I'll be there on Saturday," said Darren.

"Me too," said Eugene. "Just think, thousands of people will be watching you."

"*Thousands?*" said Bertie.

He had no idea. When the school team played, only two parents came to watch. Being Rovers' mascot was even better than he'd thought – he'd be

Dirty Bertie

famous! People would stop him in the street to ask for his autograph. He might even wear his lion costume to school for a few weeks.

CHAPTER 3

The week before the big game passed slowly. Bertie drove his family mad with what he called his "lion practice". He woke his parents early in the morning with his roaring. He made Suzy scream by jumping out from behind the bathroom door. At mealtimes he even took to eating like a lion.

Dirty Bertie

"Bertie, use your knife and fork," sighed Mum.

"I can't," said Bertie. "Lions eat with their paws."

"Not in this house, and don't slobber when you eat."

"Shlurp, shlurp!" said Bertie, licking his plate.

Dad shook his head. "I wish I'd never mentioned Larry Lion," he groaned.

On Saturday Dad drove Bertie to the Rovers stadium.

"Just do what they tell you and try not to get overexcited," he warned.

Bertie didn't see how it was possible to be *overexcited*. After all, he was going to be a lion!

Dirty Bertie

At the ground they were shown into the manager's office. Barry Ball was a big bulldog of a man with a firm handshake.

"So, Bertie, you like football, do you?" he asked.

"Yes," replied Bertie. "And I'm pretty good at roaring."

"Roaring?" said the manager, looking confused.

Dirty Bertie

"He's been excited all week about dressing up as Larry Lion," Dad explained.

"I'm sure that won't be necessary," laughed Barry Ball. "Let's go downstairs and you can meet the lads."

In the dressing room Bertie was introduced to the Rovers' players. To him they all looked like giants. The captain was called Kyle.

"Bertie, put it there!" said Kyle, giving him a high five. "Let's find you a Rovers kit, shall we?"

Dirty Bertie

Bertie changed into the Rovers yellow shirt and shorts. It looked good but he was keen to see the rest of his costume.

"What about my lion's head?" he asked.

Barry Ball smiled. "That's what I was saying, you don't have to wear a costume," he said. "Anyway, it's far too big."

"It's okay, I'd *like* to wear it," said Bertie.

"Yes, but that's Tommy's job. He's Larry Lion but he's off with a bad back this week," explained the manager. "Anyway, you look fine in football kit."

Bertie's shoulders drooped. After all his practice, they didn't want him to be the lion. It was so unfair. He'd set his heart on wearing the costume and

Dirty Bertie

a boring football kit wasn't the same.
Worst of all, his friends would think he'd
made the whole thing up.

Dirty Bertie

"I'd better get to my seat," said Dad. "Try to stay out of trouble, Bertie, and I'll see you at half-time."

Bertie sat kicking his legs while the players got changed. He wondered where they kept the lion costume. It must be somewhere if Tommy wasn't wearing it. He peeped into the next room and noticed a row of grey lockers. Maybe he'd just take a little look around…

The first three lockers were empty but in the next he struck gold. A lion costume hung on a hook, complete with a gigantic head. Surely there was no harm in just trying it on? Quickly, he slipped into the suit and pulled on the head. He could just see out through a gap in the mouth.

"Hey, Bertie, where are you?" called
Barry Ball. "We're ready to go!"

Uh oh, they were calling him. Bertie
looked at his huge furry feet and paws.
There wasn't time to take off the
costume, he'd just have to go as he was.
He plodded back into the dressing room.

Dirty Bertie

When the players saw him they all burst out laughing.

"I told you, it's way too big for you!" said Barry Ball.

"Oh, let him wear it, boss," grinned Kyle. "Who's going to know it's not Tommy?"

He took Bertie's paw and led him out. Bertie heard the clatter of football studs as they went down a long tunnel. Ahead he could see bright lights and hear music playing. They stepped out into the vast stadium. This was it...

CHAPTER 4

A great roar from the crowd greeted
the teams. Bertie glowed with pride
and waved a paw. The players ran off
to warm up, kicking a ball to each other.
Bertie stood waving to everyone. He
hoped that Darren and Eugene could
see him.

THUMP! A football landed at his feet.

Dirty Bertie

"Go on. Take a shot, Bertie," said
Kyle.

Bertie wasn't brilliant at shooting and
he was wearing giant furry feet. Still,
thousands of people were watching.
He ran at the ball and hoofed it with
all his might. It missed the goal but hit
someone on the back. The "someone"
turned round and glared at him — it was
the referee.

Dirty Bertie

"Oops, sorry!" cried Bertie. He danced away swishing his tail.

Bertie joined the teams as they lined up. He shook the City players' hands and they shook him by the paw. Then the referee blew his whistle to start the game and Bertie's starring role was over.

He stood on the sidelines watching the ball zip back and forth. It was hard to see much from inside the lion's head. After about twenty minutes, he heard a big cheer. Bertie looked round and saw the ball in the back of the net. GOAL! He jumped up and down and did his lion dance. But hang on a minute – the Rovers players were all holding their heads in their hands. The ball was in *their* goal – it was City who'd scored!

A hand tapped him on the shoulder.

Dirty Bertie

It was the linesman with his yellow flag.

"I can't see the game with your big head in the way," he grumbled.

"But I'm the mascot!" said Bertie.

"I don't care who you are, stand over there behind the goal."

Bertie trailed off. He didn't see why he couldn't stand wherever he wanted.

"BERTIE! HEY, BERTIE!"

Bertie turned round. Darren and Eugene were calling and waving from the crowd. Bertie waved back. Then he did his lion dance, waggling his bottom and making his tail swing round and round.

"HEY!" shouted the linesman. "For the last time, keep away from the pitch!"

Bertie sighed. There was no pleasing some people.

At half-time, Dad arrived to check
how he was getting on. The referee
came over and gave Bertie a lecture
about not standing near the touchline.

"Sorry. He's never been a mascot before," Dad explained. "He just gets a bit overexcited."

The second half began. Bertie stood behind the City goal, trying to keep out of the way. The game seemed to be going nowhere. The crowd had gone quiet and Rovers were heading for a 1-0 defeat. As the mascot Bertie felt he ought to help. Perhaps if he danced or did a cartwheel the crowd would make more noise? He tried a cartwheel but it was more of a bad head over heels. He tried it again then spun round waving his tail. When he stopped, he found he'd made himself dizzy. He staggered a few steps to one side.

"HEY! GET OFF THE PITCH, YOU IDIOT!"

Dirty Bertie

The linesman was shouting again.
Bertie swung round…

THUD!

Something thumped him hard on the side of the head.

A split second later there was a deafening roar. Bertie sat up. The ball was in the net and the City goalkeeper was face down on the grass. For a moment Bertie couldn't think what had happened. Then a scrum of Rovers players were jumping on top of him.

"Great goal, Bertie!" said Kyle.

Bertie realized he'd wandered on
to the pitch. The ball must have hit his
head and bounced into the goal. He'd
scored for Rovers!

The goal caused an almighty row. The
City players crowded round the referee
arguing and pointing. The referee went
over to the linesman. Finally, he gave

the goal because he couldn't think of anything in the rules about lions.

Bertie's moment of glory didn't last long however. The referee sent him off to a chorus of boos. Bertie waved one last time as he trudged off. It wasn't *his* fault the ball had hit him. He'd never even seen it!

Ten minutes later the whistle went and the game ended in a draw. The Rovers fans cheered while the City fans booed the referee loudly.

Bertie stood by the tunnel as the Rovers players came off. They all shook his hand or clapped him on the back.

"Nice header, Bertie! We should sign you up!" said Kyle.

Dirty Bertie

Bertie took off his lion's head and costume. His face was hot but he was grinning.

Dad arrived looking flustered.

"Can I be mascot again next week?" Bertie asked.

"I think maybe once was enough," said Dad.

"Anyway, Tommy will be wanting his job back," added Barry Ball.

The referee was still red-faced and arguing with the City players. When he caught sight of Bertie he pushed past them.

"Uh oh, I think he's coming over," said Dad. "Time we were going, Bertie. Come on!"

They left the ground and hurried to the car park.

Dirty Bertie

Bertie looked down. In the race to get away he'd forgotten to remove his giant furry lion's feet.

"Oh well," he said. "You never know when I might need them."

SWOT CAMP!

CHAPTER 1

Bertie strolled home, swinging his bag. *At last, the summer holidays!* he thought. Six whole weeks without lessons, homework or Miss Boot telling him to stop talking. Stuffed in his bag was a leaflet that she'd handed out at home time. Bertie hadn't bothered paying much attention – letters from school were usually boring.

Back home he settled down in front of the TV. Mum came in.

"What's this?" she asked, waving the leaflet. "I found it in your bag."

"Oh yes, Miss Boot gave it to us," said Bertie. "It's a camp or something – I wasn't really listening."

BRIGHT SPARKS CAMP

Make friends and have fun learning with other bright sparks!

Dirty Bertie

Mum read it through. Bertie had
never been on a summer camp and
this one sounded educational. He
certainly needed to do something
about his school marks. His last report
said: "Bertie's work has actually gone
backwards this year."

"This sounds fun, Bertie," she said.
"Would you like to go?"

"ME?" said Bertie.

"Yes, it'll give you
something to do in the
holidays," said Mum.

Dirty Bertie

Bertie thought he had plenty to do already. For starters, there were a million TV shows he wanted to watch.

"I'll be busy," he said.

"It's only for a week," said Mum. "I expect there'll be lots of games and activities. You might even learn something."

Bertie frowned. He wouldn't mind learning how to jet ski but that seemed unlikely.

"No thanks, I'd rather stay at home," he said.

"But you might enjoy it," Mum persisted. "Don't you want to make some new friends?"

"I like my *old* friends," replied Bertie. "Anyway, when we went camping it rained all the time and the toilets stunk."

"Summer camp's not like that," said
Mum. "I expect you sleep in rooms with
comfy beds."

"I like sleeping in my *own* bed," said
Bertie.

He didn't see why Mum was so keen
for him to go to summer camp. Anyone
would think she wanted to get rid of
him!

Dad came in.

Dirty Bertie

"Take a look at this," said Mum. "I thought Bertie might like to go."

"I wouldn't!" said Bertie.

"It sounds great," said Dad. "I wish *I'd* had the chance to go to summer camp."

"But I'd rather stay here with my friends," argued Bertie.

"Well maybe Darren or Eugene would like to go?" suggested Mum. "I could speak to their parents."

Bertie sighed. He wished Miss Boot had never given out the leaflets!

Later that evening Mum found Bertie in his room.

"Darren can't go but Eugene's parents love the idea," she reported. "So it's all agreed, you two are off to camp."

Bertie sighed. He didn't seem to have much choice in the matter.

CHAPTER 2

At the weekend Bertie discussed the camp with his friends.

"It's not fair!" grumbled Darren, "I never get to go anywhere!"

"You're lucky, I didn't ask to go," said Bertie. "My parents practically made me."

"At least we'll both be there," said

47

Eugene. "Maybe they've got a swimming pool."

"My cousin says summer camp is fantastic," said Darren. "He did rock climbing and zip wiring. Every night they cooked over a campfire."

"Really?" said Bertie. The leaflet hadn't said anything about zip wires or rock climbing.

"You'll have a great time while I'm stuck at home," grumbled Darren.

"My parents keep saying I might learn something," said Bertie. "What does that mean?"

On the first Monday of the holidays, Bertie and Eugene waited for the coach to arrive. Bertie had never been away

from his family before. He couldn't
imagine how they'd cope without him.
He stared at the other campers, waiting
with their parents. They all looked smart
and well behaved. Strangely, a number
of them were clutching pencil cases.

"Who are all these kids?"
whispered Bertie.

Eugene shrugged. "They must be
from other schools," he said. "It
doesn't look like anyone else
from our school's going."

Dirty Bertie

At last the coach arrived. The man in charge was called Mr Twig, who made them line up.

"Be good, Bertie," said Dad.

"I'm sure you'll have a wonderful time," said Mum, hugging him.

"Try not to work too hard," grinned Suzy.

Bertie frowned. This was a holiday – he wasn't planning to do any work!

On the coach he settled into a seat next to Eugene. At the last minute a boy climbed on, looking out of breath. Bertie glanced up.

"OH NO! Not Know-All Nick!" he groaned.

Nick was the last person he wanted at camp. He ducked down in his seat but it was too late.

"Oh hello, Bertie!" Nick sneered. "Don't tell me *you're* coming to camp?"

"I was, until *you* arrived," replied Bertie.

"I go to Bright Sparks every summer," boasted Nick. "In fact it was me who told Miss Boot about it. Mum says it's good for me to mix with other clever children."

Dirty Bertie

Bertie rolled his eyes.

"I thought you'd hate summer camp," said Eugene. "You don't even like games or sports."

"Sports?" Nick sniggered. "Oh no, I think you've got the wrong idea. It's not *that* sort of summer camp."

"Then what sort is it?" asked Bertie.

"Bright Sparks is a summer school for clever children," said Nick. "We do maths, science, spelling – all my favourite things in fact. I'm sure *you're* going to love it, Bertie!"

A *summer school* – with children like Nick? Bertie felt a wave of panic. He looked around wildly but the coach was moving off. Suddenly it all made sense. No wonder Miss Boot was keen to hand out the leaflets. No wonder his parents

Dirty Bertie

wanted him to go. He'd been tricked!
Bright Sparks was a school for swots!
He stared at his fellow campers on the
bus, clutching their new pencil cases.
This was all a terrible mistake.

"STOP THE BUS!" he wailed. "I want
to get off!"

CHAPTER 3

The coach turned down a long drive and came to a stop. Bertie stared at an ancient school topped with turrets and towers. It looked older than his gran.

"At least we won't be sleeping in tents," said Eugene.

"No, but we're back at school!" moaned Bertie.

Dirty Bertie

Nick poked him in the back. "I hope you're not going to moan all the time," he said. "Bright Sparks always look on the bright side."

Mr Twig took them up to their dormitory. Iron beds sat in two rows in a dark, chilly room. Notices on the walls said:

"Tidy children have tidy minds" and *"Bright sparks always give their best!"*

"Well, this is home for the week," said Mr Twig. "You've got half an hour to make your beds and fold your clothes before assembly."

Bertie had never made a bed in his life. Summer camp was like joining the army!

Downstairs they filed into the grand hall under the eye of the teachers. The campers sat up straight and folded their

arms. Miss Cram, the
camp director, stood up
and beamed.

"Welcome campers,
old and new," she said.
"Some summer camps
are all about idle pleasure
– swimming, campfires
and zip wires, that kind
of thing. Bright Sparks
is different. If you enjoy
hard work and getting top
marks then you've come
to the right place."

"Hooray!" cheered
Nick.

"Help!" gulped Eugene.

"Get me out of here!"
moaned Bertie.

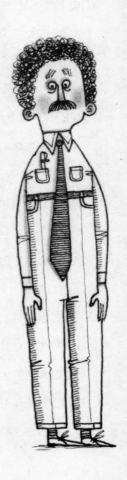

"Now I'm sure you want to see your timetables, so Mr Twig will hand them out," Miss Cram went on.

Bertie was given a timetable with his name on. The day began with "Fun with maths", followed by spelling, grammar, science, more maths (advanced) and a test to round off the day.

"I love tests!" chirped Nick. "It's just like school!"

"No," said Bertie. "It's even worse."

At least at school they got to go home. Here there was no escape from teachers all day and night. Where were the zip wires and campfires Darren had talked about? Nick leaned closer.

"So aren't you glad you came, Bertie?" he smirked.

Bertie ground his teeth.

Dirty Bertie

$$+ \ - \ \times \ \div$$

At 7 a.m. the next morning he was
woken by a loud bell. Bertie opened his
eyes and remembered. Oh no, he was
stuck at swot camp and a long day of
lessons lay ahead of him.

"Couldn't your mum come and fetch
us?" he begged Eugene as they got dressed.

"No chance," said Eugene. "I bet they
knew all along this was a swot camp."

Bertie trailed from one lesson to the
next. Sometimes they took place outdoors
but that meant marching round the field,
chanting their times tables. With Miss
Comma they played spelling games. You
moved up a place if you spelled a word
correctly and down a place if you got it
wrong. Bertie sunk quickly to the bottom.

Dirty Bertie

Know-All Nick passed him in the corridor.

"Having fun, Bertie?" he jeered. "Can you spell 'Dumbo' yet?"

"Can you spell, 'Get Lost'?" Bertie replied.

Back at the dorm, Bertie lay on his bed. "It's torture!" he groaned.

"I know," said Eugene. "And the worst thing is we're meant to be on holiday!"

Bertie sighed. Six more days of lessons, tests and Nick's ugly face at breakfast. There had to be a way out.

"I know," he said. "We could escape!"

"How?" asked Eugene. "We're miles from anywhere!"

This was true enough. Even if they got out of school they'd probably get lost in the woods. Bertie sat up.

"Wait, what if they *sent* us home?" he said.

"Why would they do that?" asked Eugene.

"They might if we broke the rules," said Bertie. "What if we did something so awful that they'd have to get rid of us?"

Eugene looked anxious. He hated getting into trouble. But Bertie's mind was already racing ahead. What crime would be so bad that Miss Cram would be forced to send them home?

CHAPTER 4

Bertie lay awake half the night but nothing came to him until the following day. In the afternoon Mr Twig was taking them for a nature lesson as part of science.

"I want you each to take one of these jars," he said. "Let's see what insects you can collect for us to study. Caterpillars, slugs, ladybirds, beetles — anything you can find."

Bertie couldn't believe his luck. Finally, this was his kind of lesson — he loved any sort of creepy-crawly. And better still, it had given him a brilliant idea.

Bertie grabbed a jar and followed Eugene outside. They found a rock and rolled it over. Underneath dozens of shiny black beetles crawled around.

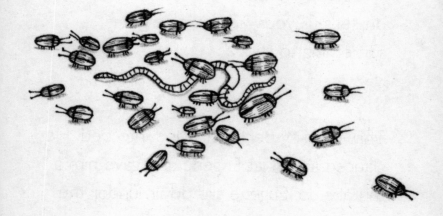

"Perfect," said Bertie, scooping some into his jar. He checked no one was watching and hid the jar under a bush.

"What are you doing?" asked Eugene. "We're meant to take that back to class."

"No one will notice," said Bertie. "We can pick it up at the end. You want to get sent home, don't you?"

"Well, yes," said Eugene. "But how are beetles going to help?"

"I'll explain later," said Bertie. "Come on, let's fill your jar so we've got something to show."

That evening Bertie crawled into bed. He glanced across at Eugene and gave him a thumbs up. Eugene slid down under the covers. He could hardly bear to watch.

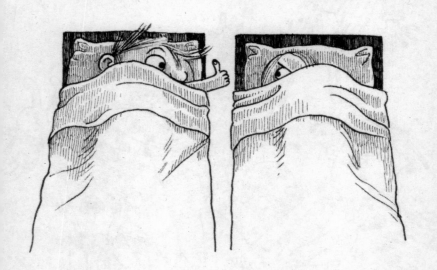

"Lights out, children, no talking," said Mr Twig. The room was plunged into darkness. Bertie waited. It shouldn't be too long now. Three, two, one…

"YEEEARGHHH!" a boy screamed. "There's something in my bed!"

"HEEELP!" yelled another. "It's crawling up my leg!"

The lights went back on. All over the dorm, boys were leaping out of bed and hopping around as if their pyjamas were on fire.

Mr Twig saw something black scuttle across the floor and trapped it in his hand.

"Hmm. A ground beetle," he said. "I wonder how that got in?"

He looked around. Only two boys had remained in their beds. One was hiding under the covers while the other seemed to be enjoying the chaos.

"Bertie," said Mr Twig. "Come here. You too, Eugene."

Bertie got out of bed. "Now we're in big trouble!" he grinned.

Early next morning Bertie and Eugene waited outside Miss Cram's office.

"Don't look so worried," whispered Bertie. "She'll probably tell us off, then send us home."

Miss Cram opened the door and beckoned them in.

"Ah, our two practical jokers," she said, taking a seat at her desk. "Mr Twig told

me about your little prank. I suppose
you think putting beetles in someone's
bed is funny?"

"Quite funny," said Bertie.

Miss Cram glared. "We do not tolerate
troublemakers at this camp," she said. "I
am very tempted to send you home."

Whoopee! thought Bertie. *Goodbye
swot camp!*

"However I don't believe in giving up
on children," Miss Cram went on. "So I've
decided to move you to another dorm."

Bertie gaped.

"M-move us?" he stammered.

"That's what I said. I've asked one of
our trusted campers to keep a close eye
on you," said Miss Cram. "He'll be with
you every minute of the day to make
sure you behave."

Dirty Bertie

There was a knock on the door.
Bertie looked round. His face fell.

"Hello, Bertie!" smirked Know-All
Nick. "We're going to have so much fun
together!"

ROBOT WARS!

BOOTOSAURUS

Weight:	15kg
Dimensions:	27cm x 84cm x 75cm
Power:	Secret
Weapons:	Flip-up lid
Strengths:	Unpredictable
Weaknesses:	Unpredictable

CHAPTER 1

Hooray! Miss Boot was away on a course, which meant Mr Weakly was teaching Bertie's class this week.

"Now settle down everyone," pleaded Mr Weakly, clapping his hands.

Bertie aimed a ball of paper at Know-All Nick's head. This was going to be brilliant. Mr Weakly was as timid as a mouse. He didn't seem to notice when Bertie turned round or balanced a ruler on his head. Better still, it was easy to distract him by asking questions like, "Have you got a girlfriend?" Mr Weakly turned as red as a beetroot if you asked him that.

"I have some exciting news," said Mr Weakly. "In three weeks I'm planning to enter a team for the Junior Science Challenge. Who wants to take part?"

Stony silence.

"This year's challenge is to build a robot for a battle of the robots contest," squeaked Mr Weakly.

A robot? Bertie's hand shot up with everyone else's. His favourite programme on TV was *Robot Wars*, where robots battled like gladiators. Building a robot would be a dream come true.

"Goodness!" said Mr Weakly. "I'm afraid I can't take all of you. Write down your names and I'll try to pick a team."

After the lesson Bertie and his friends waited to add their names to the list.

"He has to choose us," said Bertie.

Darren pulled a face. "I bet he only takes teacher's pets like Know-All Nick," he said.

"I heard that!" cried Nick, turning round. "Anyway, *you* don't stand a chance, Bertie. Don't forget, you're the one who locked Mr Weakly in the store cupboard."

"Only because Darren dared me," said Bertie.

"Still, it's probably not going to help," sighed Eugene.

"Just let me talk to him," said Bertie. "We've got to be on that team."

Mr Weakly was packing away his books.

"Scuse me, sir," began Bertie. "We're dead interested in robots."

"Well, ah yes, me too," smiled Mr Weakly.

"What I mean is we'd be perfect for the team," said Bertie.

"I'm sure you would," said Mr Weakly. "But I have all the other children to consider as well."

Dirty Bertie

"I know," said Bertie. "But obviously you'll want to pick the ones who come top at science. And that's Eugene, Darren and me."

"Really?" said Mr Weakly. He couldn't picture Bertie coming top at anything.

"Imagine if we actually won the competition," Bertie went on. "Miss Boot would be dead impressed – and Miss Skinner, too!"

"Well yes, I hadn't thought of that," admitted Mr Weakly.

Dirty Bertie

It was true he wasn't Miss Skinner's favourite member of staff – mainly because his classes did what they liked.

"Well anyway, it's up to you," said Bertie. "But our names are on the list – Darren, Eugene and Bertie. I've underlined them."

Eugene closed the door behind them.

"What did you tell him that for?" he groaned. "We've never ever come top in science!"

"No, but *he* doesn't know that," grinned Bertie. "If it gets us in the team then that's all that matters."

CHAPTER 2

The next morning Mr Weakly read out the team for the competition.

"Amanda Thribb and Nicholas," he began.

Nick shot Bertie a look of triumph.

"And the rest of the team will be … Darren, Eugene and Bertie," added Mr Weakly.

Dirty Bertie

Nick gasped. Bertie almost fell off his chair. They'd done it — they were in the science team!

This was going to be amazing, thought Bertie. With a little help from Mr Weakly, they were going to build the greatest robot ever!

"We don't have much time," said Mr Weakly. "So I'd like you all to design a robot for your homework. We'll let the class decide which is the best."

Dirty Bertie

For once, Bertie couldn't wait to start on his homework. He watched *Robot Wars* every week so his head was bursting with ideas. On the way home Darren and Eugene couldn't talk about anything else.

"You wait till you see my robot," said Darren. "It's going to play football."

"I'm making Spiderbot, which climbs up tall buildings," said Eugene. "What are you doing, Bertie?"

"I haven't decided yet," replied Bertie. "But it's going to be brilliant."

Back home he sat at the kitchen table with a pencil and paper. His robot had to be fast, strong and as deadly as a scorpion. It would make other robots tremble at the knees. *Let's see,* he thought. *What would be really scary?* Suddenly he had the perfect idea...

Dirty Bertie

The next day Bertie and the others handed in their homework. Mr Weakly glanced through the drawings.

"Hmm … uh huh … good grief!" he gasped when he saw Bertie's picture. "It's rather fierce!"

"That's the idea," said Bertie. "Bootosaurus will make the other robots all run away."

Dirty Bertie

"I can't say I blame them," nodded Mr Weakly.

The picture reminded him of someone but he couldn't think who it was.

"Well, let's show these to the class," he said.

Bertie stood at the front with the others and waited for his chance to explain his idea.

Dirty Bertie

"Right, let's take a vote," said Mr Weakly, handing out slips of paper. "Write down the robot you like best and I'll tot up the results."

Bertie crossed his fingers as Mr Weakly counted.

"Well, we have a winner," he said. "Darren has five votes, Eugene four, Nick ... none, I'm afraid, Amanda eight and Bertie ... fourteen. That means Bertie's robot is the winner."

"YESSSS!" whooped Bertie.

"NOOO!" wailed Nick.

"Oh dear!" sighed Mr Weakly.

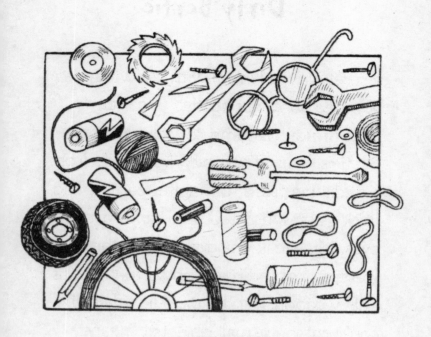

CHAPTER 3

For the next few weeks sounds of banging and hammering came from Mr Weakly's room after school. The team brought in bike lights, batteries, wheels, rubber bands and anything that might be useful. None of them had any idea how to build a robot, but luckily Mr Weakly turned out to be a whizz with a screwdriver. Finally, with a few days to go, the robot was ready.

Bootosaurus came roughly up to Bertie's waist. The body was made from a pedal bin fixed to a skateboard. It had thick glasses, pointed teeth and mad eyes. Mr Weakly said that flamethrowers were out of the question so the robot's only weapon was a flip-up lid which could catapult small objects.

Dirty Bertie

On the day of the Science Challenge, they arrived at the Pudsley Arena.

Bertie was excited to see Danny Dent from *Robot Wars* was the host.

"Woah! Check out these robots!" said Danny, looking around the hall.

"Don't worry, Bootosaurus will beat them," said Bertie.

"In your dreams," sneered Nick. "Isn't that Swotter House over there?"

Bertie recognized their old enemies who they'd beaten in the Junior Quiz.

Dirty Bertie

Here they were again in their smart blazers and shiny shoes, looking for revenge.

"Don't look now, they're coming over," whispered Eugene.

Miss Topping introduced her team.

"This is Giles, Miles, Tara and Harriet," she said. "And this must be *your* robot. Goodness, what an ugly thing!"

The Swotter House team tittered and nudged each other.

"Take a look at *our* robot," boasted Giles. "We call it Shark Attack."

"It's totally invincible," bragged Tara. "That means it can't be beaten."

Bertie stared. Shark Attack was bigger than him! And it was armed with more weapons than a battleship.

"Well, good luck," said Miss Topping. "We'll be seeing you in the final round."

"The battle to the death," said Tara. "We're looking forward to that *very much*."

They marched off with their snooty noses in the air.

"Did you see their robot?" moaned Darren. "It's built like a tank!"

"Size doesn't mean anything," said Bertie. "Bootosaurus can beat them."

"Well, if we lose we'll know who to blame," said Nick.

The competition began. Danny Dent explained the first three rounds would test the robots' speed, agility and accuracy. The final round was a battle, with the last robot standing the winner.

Round one was a race round a track. Mr Weakly said they would take it in turns on the controls with Nick going first.

Shark Attack zoomed off like a streak of lightning. Bootosauraus shot backwards because Nick hit the wrong button. They trailed in second from last.

Dirty Bertie

Things didn't improve on the agility course. Amanda crashed into every obstacle and limped in fourth. Robot Golf went better although Darren and Eugene took eighteen attempts to guide a ball into a hole. Shark Attack did it in four.

After three rounds, Swotter House sat proudly at the top of the leader board. Pudsley lay back in third – second from bottom. They needed a win to stand any chance of claiming the trophy.

They broke for lunch.

"At least we're not last," said Eugene, helping himself to a slice of pizza.

"Only because Dinosnore fell over every time," said Darren.

"Shark Attack will win easily," sniffed Know-All Nick. "It's the best robot by miles. Bertie's idea was rubbish."

"It's not over yet," argued Bertie. "We've still got our secret weapon."

"Oh yes, I forgot, the flip-up lid! *Genius!*" sneered Nick.

"At least I won't steer us *backwards*," replied Bertie.

"Boys, boys, let's not argue!" sighed Mr Weakly. "We can only try our best!"

Bertie bit into his Cheesy Feast Pizza. Nick was right – Shark Attack was bigger, stronger and had better weapons. It boasted a pincer arm and a bludger blade. Bootosaurus' flip-up lid was no use at all ... *or was it?*

Bertie stared at the gooey cheese pizza in his hand. It was a long shot but it might just work.

"Listen, Darren," he said. "Here's the plan..."

CHAPTER 4

A loud fanfare played as the robots
entered the arena for the final round.
Bertie clutched the remote controls.

Danny Dent's voice boomed over
the microphone.

"So we come to the final round
where our robots do battle. Remember,
the last robot standing wins the round

and there are double points up for grabs."

"Good luck, Bertie!" said Mr Weakly.

"Don't mess it up," hissed Nick.

Bertie watched Shark Attack spin round in circles, showing off. He'd have to keep clear of that pincer arm and bludger blade. He nodded to Darren who gave him a thumbs up.

"Robot Masters, are you ready?" asked Danny Dent. "Three, two, one… GO!"

The robots came whizzing out of their corners. Shark Attack slammed straight into Dragobot, sending it tumbling into the pit. The Swotter House team cheered wildly. Tara's eyes glinted like steel. This was going to be a breeze.

Bertie kept Bootosaurus to the edge of the arena, well out of trouble.

"What are you playing at Bertie?"
moaned Nick. "ATTACK!"

Shark Attack was back on the
warpath again, eyeing its next victim.
It grabbed Dinosnore in its pincer claw
and tossed it aside like a used hanky.

Before long, the arena was littered
with crushed and mangled robots.
Dinosnore lay upside down, Dragobot

was in the pit and Crackerjack was on fire. Only Bootosaurus remained to face the might of Shark Attack.

"Now we're for it," gulped Eugene.

Miss Topping leaned forwards and narrowed her eyes.

"Finish them, Tara," she ordered. "Remember the Junior Quiz."

Shark Attack closed in for the kill with its pincer arm raised. Bertie waited until he had Bootosaurus directly below them.

"NOW!" he cried.

Darren dropped something – a large slice of Cheesy Feast Pizza. It landed on top of Bootosaurus and Bertie quickly hit a button on the controls. The robot's lid flipped up, catapulting the pizza through the air.

SPLAT!

The gooey pizza landed
in front of Shark Attack.

"HA! Missed!" hooted Giles.
But he spoke too soon. As
Shark Attack drove over the pizza, its
wheels and axles became jammed with
gooey sticky cheese.

"Reverse, reverse, Tara!" screamed
Miss Topping in a frenzy.

But Bertie hadn't finished. He pushed
a lever. Bootosaurus shot forwards at top
speed and slammed into Shark Attack. It
skidded backwards towards the gaping
pit. For a moment it wobbled, then it
toppled in with a crash.

A huge cheer went up from the
audience. Bertie breathed out.

Dirty Bertie

"The winner of the final round with double points is Bootosaurus!" declared Danny Dent. "Which means Pudsley are this years' Junior Science Challenge winners!"

"We did it!" cried Eugene. "We actually won!"

"I knew we would all along," lied Know-All Nick.

Bertie looked at the Swotter House team arguing among themselves. Some people were just sore losers.

Dirty Bertie

The following Monday Bertie sat in the hall for a special assembly. Miss Skinner clasped her hands together.

"I'm very proud to tell you that Mr Weakly's team have won the Junior Science Challenge," she said. "I'd like them to come up now with their robot and Miss Boot will present the trophy."

Everyone cheered and clapped wildly. Bertie beamed – he'd never won a science trophy before.

Miss Boot shook Mr Weakly's hand.

"Well done all of you," she said. "And is this the robot you built for the competition? Does it have a name?"

Bertie gulped. His teammates stared at the floor.

Dirty Bertie

"It was actually Bertie's design," explained Mr Weakly. "He called it *Bootosaurus*."

"REALLY?" said Miss Boot coldly. "Tell me, Bertie, what gave you that idea?"

Dirty Bertie

SPIDER!

For Corban McBride and Skye Russell ~ D R
For Grace Styles ~ A M

Contents

SPIDER!

CHAPTER 1

"YAAAARGHHH!"

Mum's scream made Bertie drop his spoon in his Wheeto Flakes. He rushed upstairs to find his family on the landing.

Mum was standing outside the bathroom wrapped in a towel.

"There's a spider in the bath!" she cried.

"Is that all?" Dad laughed. "I thought it

was something serious!"

"You haven't seen the spider," said
Mum.

Suzy shuddered. "UGH! I hate
spiders."

"Can I see it?" begged Bertie.

"No, you keep out of the way, Bertie,
I'll deal with this," said Dad.

He marched into the bathroom.
A moment later he marched back out
again, looking shaken.

Dirty Bertie

"That's a *really* big spider," he admitted.

"I told you," said Mum. "Well, aren't you going to do something?"

"Yes, you can't just leave it in the bath," said Suzy.

"Okay, okay, I'm working on it," replied Dad. It wasn't that he was scared of spiders, he just wasn't very keen on picking them up.

"I can catch it for you!" cried Bertie.

Mum and Dad looked at each other. Clearly neither of them were about to go back in and tackle the spider.

"Well, okay," sighed Dad. "But for goodness' sake don't let it escape."

Bertie hurried off to fetch his school lunch box. It was the perfect size for a spider trap. He crept into the bathroom on tiptoe.

Dirty Bertie

"WOAH! It's massive!" he cried.

"Just get rid of it," groaned Mum. "And *hurry up, I'm freezing to death*!"

The spider was sitting halfway up the bath. It was dark, hairy and almost as big as Bertie's hand. Bertie wasn't scared of spiders though, and this one was a real whopper. Maybe it was a rare species – a King Kong spider or a giant vampire spider perhaps?

Bertie got into the bath with his lunch box at the ready.

"It's okay, Mr Spider, I won't hurt you," he whispered.

SLAM! He brought down the box. The spider made a run for it but Bertie

Dirty Bertie

was too quick for him.

"GOT YOU!" he cried, jamming on
the lid.

His family were waiting outside.

"Well? Did you get it?" asked Suzy.

"Yes," said Bertie, holding up the box.
"Look, he's a monster!"

Dirty Bertie

"EWWW!" yelled Suzy.

"Take it away!" shrieked Mum.

Bertie couldn't see what all the fuss was about. It was only a spider – anyone would think it was a man-eating python or something!

"Please, just get rid of it," said Dad.

"Can't I keep it?" asked Bertie.

"NO!" cried everyone at once.

"Just for a few days?" pleaded Bertie. "I've never had a pet spider."

"Absolutely not," said Mum. "And before you get any ideas, don't try hiding it in your room."

"Let it go in the garden," said Dad. "And then you better get off to school."

Bertie sighed. You'd think his parents would be pleased he wanted to look after a poor homeless spider. Weren't

they always saying he should be kind to
all living creatures?

He took the lunch box out to the
front garden and removed the lid.

"Sorry, Mr Spider, I'm not allowed to
keep you," he sighed.

The spider clung to the bottom of
the box.

Dirty Bertie

It was a pity no one at school would ever see him, thought Bertie. Darren and Eugene would be dead impressed. Know-All Nick would probably faint with fright. It was no use though, his mean parents refused to have the spider in the house. But hang on a moment, they hadn't said anything about *other* houses. Bertie smiled and replaced the lid. All he needed was someone to look after his spider for a little while – and luckily he knew just the person.

CHAPTER 2

DING DONG!

Bertie rang Gran's doorbell. He was late for school but this wouldn't take a minute.

Gran answered the door wearing her dressing gown.

"Bertie, what are you doing here?" she asked. "Is something the matter?"

"No, I just wanted to ask you something," replied Bertie.

"Can't it wait?" sighed Gran. "I've only just got up."

"It's sort of urgent," said Bertie. "Can you look after something for me?"

He held out the plastic lunch box. The lid had rows of tiny air holes, which Bertie had made with a fork. Gran could see a dark something moving inside.

"What is it?" she asked. "It's not a mouse?"

"Of course not, it's my pet spider," said Bertie. "I'm calling him Tickler."

"Let's have a look then," said Gran. She took the box a little cautiously and lifted the lid.

"WAAAH!" She dropped it quickly. "Are you trying to scare me to death?"

Bertie picked up the box and scooped
Tickler inside.

"I found him in the bath," he
explained. "Or actually Mum found him
but she won't let me keep him."

"I'm not surprised," said Gran.

"So anyway, can you look after him
for a bit?" asked Bertie.

Dirty Bertie

"Not likely!" said Gran. "I'm not having that thing in the house. It'll give me nightmares. Why can't you have a pet hamster like other children?"

"Mum says Whiffer is enough trouble," replied Bertie.

"Well, I'm sorry, but I can't help you," said Gran. "If you want my advice, let that spider go. Now, aren't you late for school?"

Bertie put the lunch box back in his bag and trailed off down the road.

At the school gates he caught up with Darren and Eugene.

"What happened to you?" asked Eugene.

"Sorry, I had to ask my gran about something," explained Bertie. "But wait till you see what I've got."

Dirty Bertie

He brought out the lunch box and carefully lifted the lid.

Darren and Eugene stared boggle-eyed.

"WOAH! That's *ginormous*!" cried Darren.

"Where did you get him?" asked Eugene.

"He was sitting in the bath," replied Bertie. "He's called Tickler."

"Maybe he's a tarantula?" suggested Darren. "They're the biggest spiders in the universe!"

"And the deadliest," added Eugene. "Aren't tarantulas meant to be poisonous?"

"Probably," said Bertie. "I've never had one. Do you think he *is* a tarantula?"

They all stared at Tickler – who seemed quite harmless for a deadly spider. All the same, owning a pet tarantula would be brilliant, thought Bertie. His classmates would have to treat him with more respect. Know-All Nick wouldn't dare call him "bogey nose" ever again.

"Wait, you're not bringing him to school, are you?" said Eugene.

"Why not?" asked Bertie.

"Because Miss Boot will go crackers if she sees him."

"She won't see him," replied Bertie.

"Well, be careful," warned Darren. "If he *is* a tarantula, he better not escape."

"Relax," said Bertie. "It's all under control."

Obviously he wasn't going to let a giant tarantula loose in school – he wasn't *that* stupid!

CHAPTER 3

During morning lessons, Bertie kept
the lunch box under his desk where he
could keep an eye on Tickler. Eugene
had found *The Bumper Book of Bugs* on
the class bookshelf, which had a double
page on spiders. It made interesting
reading. Bertie had no idea tarantulas
were so huge and scary.

TARANTULA
(HAIRIUS BEASTUS)

Largest known spider, which can grow
as big as your dinner plate.

Diet:
grasshoppers, beetles
and other spiders

WOAH,
get me out
of here!

Yikes! thought Bertie. The spider in
the picture wasn't something you'd want
crawling up your leg. Tickler wasn't that
big but maybe he was still a baby?

At break time, Bertie and his friends
headed for a bench in the playground.
Bertie took out his lunch box.

"Don't let him out!" cried Eugene in alarm.

"I'm not," said Bertie. "I'm just checking he's all right."

"Has he eaten anything?" asked Darren.

Bertie shook his head. He'd left Tickler a piece of cheese but it was still untouched. It was a pity he didn't have any grasshoppers or beetles.

"What are you looking at?"

Bertie looked up to see Royston Rich, the biggest boaster in the class. He snapped the lid back on the box.

"If you must know it's a spider," he said. "He's called Tickler and he's a tarantula."

"OH, HA HA!" scoffed Royston. "As if you'd have a tarantula! I don't think so!"

"You haven't seen him," said Darren. "He's almost as big as your head."

Royston folded his arms. "Prove it. Let me see," he demanded.

Bertie considered it. A pet tarantula could turn out to be very useful.

"I can't let you see him for free," he said. "What have you got?"

Royston rolled his eyes. He reached into his bag and handed over a fudge bar.

Bertie put it in his pocket. Checking that no teachers were around, he lifted the lid.

"WOAH!" squawked Royston. "That's a monster!"

"Told you," said Bertie. "He's a tarantula."

"How do you know?" asked Royston.

"We read it in a book," said Darren.

Bertie decided they should have some fun with Royston.

Dirty Bertie

"Did you know that tarantulas can bite?" he asked.

"C-can they?" gulped Royston.

"Oh yes, if a tarantula bites you, your face turns yellow and all your teeth fall out," said Bertie.

Royston took a step back. "I ... um ... better be going," he said, hurrying off.

"You made that up," said Eugene.

"It wasn't in the book."

"I know," grinned Bertie, "but Royston doesn't."

This was brilliant. He could make up anything he liked and everyone would believe it.

Before long, word spread around the playground and a queue formed. Bertie was offered sweets and crisps to see the deadly tarantula.

"So where's this scary spider, then?"

Bertie smiled. He might have guessed Know-All Nick would poke his nose in sooner or later.

"He's in the box," said Bertie.

"I bet it's not a tarantula at all," sneered Nick. "It's probably just a dopey daddy-long-legs."

"It's a tarantula," said Bertie.

"Liar, liar, pants on fire!" chanted Nick.

Dirty Bertie

Bertie scowled. "Look, smelly-pants, do you want to see him or not?" he demanded.

Nick pulled a face and handed over half a jelly snake. Bertie added it to his growing pile of goodies.

"You have to come close," said Bertie. "But be careful, he might jump on you." Bertie lifted the lid as Nick peered inside.

"G-golly!" gulped Nick. "That's a big one!"

"Tarantulas are the biggest and the deadliest," said Bertie.

Nick bent his head a little closer.

"He's not moving," he said. "Are you sure he's alive?"

Dirty Bertie

"Oh, he's alive all right," said Bertie.

He tapped the box and Tickler suddenly scuttled to the other end.

"YEEAAAARGHHH!" wailed Nick, leaping back in fright. "You did that on purpose! I'm telling Miss Boot!"

"You better not," warned Bertie. "Or I might put a tarantula down your trousers."

"You wouldn't!" gasped Nick.

"Try me," said Bertie. "Do you know what happens when you're bitten by a tarantula?"

Nick didn't but he wasn't waiting to find out. He ran off as fast as he could.

Bertie took a bite of the jelly snake. This was a gold mine, he thought. With a few more Ticklers he could open a spider zoo and make a fortune!

CHAPTER 4

Back in class, everyone settled into their seats. Bertie noticed that Trevor and Amanda had moved further away from him. Clearly they weren't too keen on sharing the classroom with a tarantula. While Miss Boot wrote maths questions for the class, Bertie took the chance to check on Tickler.

Dirty Bertie

HELP! OH PANTS! OH NO! He'd escaped!

Bertie emptied out his bag on the floor. No Tickler.

"What are you doing?" asked Eugene.

"I can't find Tickler!" hissed Bertie.

"What? You're joking!"

"No! He's not in his box!" muttered Bertie.

Bertie looked under his chair with growing panic. It was one thing scaring his classmates – it was another having a tarantula loose in the classroom. What if Tickler crawled up somebody's leg? What if he actually bit them? They might really turn yellow or even drop dead on the spot! Miss Boot would guess he was to blame. Who else would bring a deadly spider into school?

Dirty Bertie

As Miss Boot droned on, Bertie slid down under his desk. There was no sign of Tickler. Bertie inched forwards on his hands and knees, searching the floor.

"Here, Tickler! Where are you?" he whispered.

"BERTIE!" boomed Miss Boot.

Bertie froze.

Now he was for it.

Dirty Bertie

"Come out from there!" ordered Miss Boot.

Bertie struggled to his feet.

"WELL?" thundered Miss Boot. "What were you doing?"

"Nothing," mumbled Bertie. "I just lost something."

"Speak up!" snapped Miss Boot. "What have you lost?"

"My um ... my pet spider," admitted Bertie.

The class gasped.

"IT'S A GIANT TARANTULA! WE'RE ALL GOING TO DIE!" wailed Nick.

Panic swept through the class as children screamed and leaped to their feet. They fled to Miss Boot, clinging to her for protection. Know-All Nick climbed on to a desk and tried to

Dirty Bertie

escape through the window. Bertie
hadn't seen chaos like this since the
time Whiffer did something in Royston's
swimming pool.

"QUIET!" thundered Miss Boot.
"Everyone calm down and look on
the floor."

Dirty Bertie

Out of the corner of his eye, Bertie saw something scuttle out from a desk. Tickler! Miss Boot saw him too. Cutting him off, she brought her hand down on the spider. The class held their breath. They waited for her to scream, turn yellow and drop dead on the spot. But Miss Boot did none of these things. She lifted Tickler up and dropped him into a plastic cup on her desk.

"For your information, Bertie, this is NOT a tarantula," she said. "Tarantulas are much bigger and they live in the rainforest. This is just a common house spider. It couldn't bite you if it tried."

"You lied!" bleated Nick. "I gave you half my jelly snake."

"And I gave you my fudge bar," said Royston.

Dirty Bertie

"Did you indeed?" said Miss Boot. "Well, I'm sure Bertie will be only too happy to return anything he took. But first I have a job for him. Come here, Bertie."

Bertie trailed out to the front.

"Take this horrid creature and get rid of it," ordered Miss Boot. "I never ever want to see it in school again."

Bertie headed down the corridor with Tickler back in his box. This time the spider would have to go for good… Or would he? At the main door Bertie paused and turned round. An idea had come to him. There was one place in school Miss Boot would never look for Tickler. And better still, Bertie would be able to visit him whenever he liked.

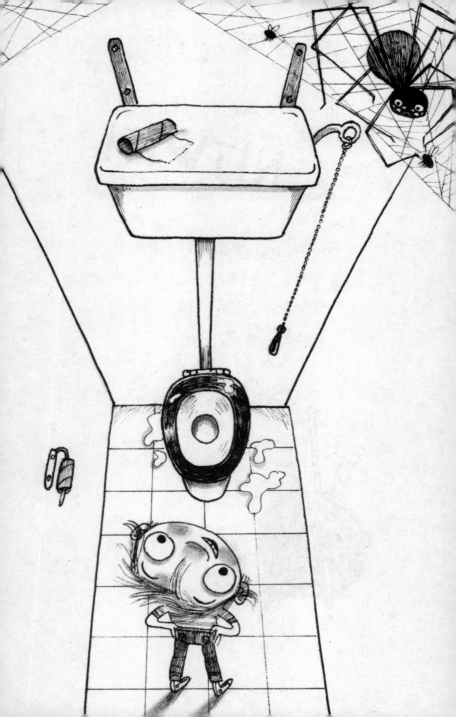

NITWIT!

CHAPTER 1

Bertie's gran often dropped round
for tea in the afternoon. Today she'd
brought along a large package wrapped
in silver paper.

"What have you got there, Gran?"
asked Suzy.

"Actually, it's a little present for
Bertie," said Gran. "I know it's a bit late

for Christmas but I hope he likes it."

A present? Bertie didn't mind getting presents at any time of year! What could it be? Maybe the Worm Farm he'd been saving up to buy or the Super Stinker Stinkbomb Kit his parents had refused to get him. He tore off the wrapping.

"A jumper," he said flatly.

"I knitted it myself," Gran smiled.

Bertie could have guessed that by the number of holes in it. He held up the huge baggy jumper, which was the colour of school custard. A row of fluffy white lambs skipped across the front. Bertie thought it was probably the worst jumper in the history of jumpers.

"Aww, isn't that lovely?" cooed Mum. "What do you say, Bertie?"

"Um, thanks, Gran," mumbled Bertie.

"Try it on!" cried Suzy eagerly.

Bertie glared at his sister – she was obviously enjoying this. Reluctantly, he pulled it on. The sleeves dangled down and it hung to his knees. It was more like a dress than a jumper!

"It's too big!" he protested.

"Nonsense, you'll soon grow into it," said Mum.

"It's meant to be big, that's the style

these days!" beamed Gran.

"And the little lambs are *so* sweet," grinned Suzy. "Why don't you wear it to school tomorrow?"

Wear it to school? You must be joking! thought Bertie.

"I'm not allowed to wear jumpers," he said. "It's against the rules."

"Don't be silly," said Mum. "You often wear a jumper to school."

"But not like this, mine are all brown!" said Bertie.

"Then it will make a nice change," said Suzy. "I bet none of your friends has got a jumper like that."

Bertie was certain they hadn't. They wouldn't be seen dead in a custard-yellow jumper with skipping lambs on the front.

Dirty Bertie

"Well, it's very kind of you, Gran," said Mum.

"Oh, it's no trouble at all," laughed Gran. "I love knitting. I could knit one for you if you like, Suzy?"

"Yes! Great idea!" cried Bertie.

"Oh no, that's okay, Gran," said Suzy quickly. "Wool makes me itchy. But I'm looking forward to Bertie wearing his new jumper to school."

Dirty Bertie

Bertie scowled. There was no way he was wearing the knitted horror to school. His friends would never stop laughing. Miss Boot would probably make him stand up in assembly to show the whole school! No, there was only one thing for it – he'd have to hide the jumper somewhere no one could find it.

CHAPTER 2

The next morning, Bertie got dressed
for school. He pulled on his pants,
jeans and T-shirt. He opened the
bottom drawer where he kept all his
jumpers.

HELP! *Where had they all gone?*
The drawer was empty! He rushed
downstairs in a panic.

Dirty Bertie

"Mum, where are all my jumpers?" he asked.

"Oh, they were dirty, so I put them in the wash," said Mum with a knowing smile.

"*ALL of them?*" cried Bertie. "But what am I going to wear to school?"

"Your new jumper of course," said Mum. "I found it under your bed. I can't think how it got there."

Dirty Bertie

"I can't wear that!" moaned Bertie.
"It's too big! It looks like a dress!"

"Don't be silly," said Mum. "Anyway,
you promised Gran you'd wear it today."

Bertie didn't remember promising
anything. This was so unfair!

He thumped back upstairs. It was a
plot. His mum had washed all his other
jumpers on purpose.

Five minutes later he was back. Mum
looked up.

"Bertie!" she said. "You can't go to
school in just a T-shirt."

"Why not?" asked Bertie.

"Because it's winter, you'll freeze to
death!" said Mum.

"I can run around!" said Bertie. "I'll
be fine."

"I'm not arguing with you," said Mum.

Dirty Bertie

"You're wearing the nice jumper Gran knitted and that's the end of it. Go and put it on."

Bertie trailed down the road to school. He was wearing the knitted horror but at least nobody could see it. He had his coat zipped up to his neck.

Eugene and Darren were waiting on the corner as usual.

"Hi, Bertie!" said Eugene. "What's that yellow thing?"

Bertie looked down. Help! The jumper was so long it was sticking out below his coat! He tried to tuck it in.

"Are you wearing a nappy?" asked Darren.

"Very funny," said Bertie. "If you must

know it's a jumper my gran knitted."

"Oh! A Granny jumper!" Darren
smiled.

"Well, let's see it then," said Eugene.

Dirty Bertie

"Yes, show us," urged Darren. "We won't laugh, will we, Eugene?"

Bertie sighed and fingered the zip on his coat. Should he? No, he couldn't face it.

"Is that the time? We'll be late for school," he said, hurrying on.

The others raced after him.

"Come on, Bertie, you can't keep your coat on all day!" said Darren.

Oh no? You just watch me, thought Bertie.

In the playground, Bertie stood with his friends, keeping his coat firmly zipped up. When the bell went they all filed into school. Bertie's classmates hung up their coats. Bertie kept his on. He sneaked into class and sat down at the back. Miss Boot was taking the register.

"Donna?" she boomed.

"Yes, Miss!"

"Nicholas?"

"Here, Miss Boot!"

"BERTIE?" Miss Boot looked up. "Bertie, why are you still wearing your coat?"

Bertie turned pink. "The zip's stuck!" he said.

"Don't talk nonsense," barked Miss Boot. "Take it off!"

"I can't! It won't budge!" wailed Bertie, pretending to tug at the zip.

Miss Boot sighed. She marched over, grabbed the zip and yanked it down.

"There!"

By now the class had all turned round to stare. Bertie gulped and slipped off his coat. His classmates giggled.

Dirty Bertie

"Ooh, nice jumper, Bertie!" jeered Royston.

Dirty Bertie

"Ahh, it's so cute!" smirked Know-All Nick. "Look at the lickle lambies!"

Bertie glared at them. "If you must know, my gran knitted it," he said.

Miss Boot's mouth twitched.

"Don't listen to them, Bertie," she said. "I think it's very er … colourful."

This set off new waves of giggles. Bertie turned pink and slumped back in his seat. This was worse than the time he had to wear a kilt for his cousin's wedding. There was only one way to put an end to it – the knitted horror would have to go. But how could he get rid of it? Suddenly it came to him. It was Thursday – they went swimming on Thursday… What better place to lose a jumper than at the swimming baths?

CHAPTER 3

The coach pulled into the car park and everyone trooped off. Darren put on his swimming goggles.

"Your jumper's so bright it's hurting my eyes," he explained.

"Very funny," scowled Bertie. "Anyway, I won't be wearing it much longer."

"Oh, why's that then?" asked Eugene.

Dirty Bertie

"Yes, why *is* that?" sneered a voice. It was Know-All Nick, his old enemy.

"Mind your own business, big nose," said Bertie.

Bertie waited until the swimming lesson was over. Now was his chance. He grabbed his clothes and slammed the locker door shut, leaving the knitted horror inside. By the time anyone found it he'd be gone. He looked around. Only Know-All Nick was about, combing his hair in a mirror.

"All right, Bertie?" he smiled slyly. "Sure you've got everything?"

Dirty Bertie

"Yes thanks," said Bertie.

Once he was dressed, he hurried to the coach and found a seat. He'd done it. *Goodbye, knitted horror!* he thought. *I won't be seeing you again!*

Mr Weakly climbed on to the coach with Know-All Nick. Bertie stared in disbelief. The teacher had something in his hand – a custard-yellow jumper.

"Has … ah … anyone lost a jumper?" he asked, holding it up.

Bertie slid down in his seat.

"Please, sir, I think it's Bertie's," Nick bleated. "He's always losing things!"

"Bertie, is this yours?" asked Mr Weakly.

"Oh yes, it's *definitely* his," said Darren.

"It's his favourite," added Eugene.

Bertie glared at them. So much for friends!

"Well, you better look after it," said Mr Weakly. "You're lucky that Nicholas found it. Aren't you going to thank him?"

Bertie ground his teeth.

"Thanks *a lot*, Nickerless," he said.

"That's all right," smirked Nick. "I'd hate you to lose your lovely new jumper. I'll have to keep an eye on it for you!"

The coach set off. Bertie glared at the
jumper in his lap. Trust Know-All Nick
to ruin everything, he thought. Why
couldn't he mind his own business?

"Nice try, Bertie. Better luck next
time," grinned Darren.

"It's all right for you," grumbled Bertie.
"You don't have to wear it."

"It's not *that* bad," said Darren.

"All right, why don't we swap?"
suggested Bertie. "I'll wear *your* jumper."

"No way!" snorted Darren. "I'm not
wearing that thing."

Bertie stared out of the window.
There had to be some way to get rid of
the knitted horror. Suddenly it came to
him. It was simple — all he had to do was
leave it on the coach when he got off.

Ten minutes later, the coach pulled up

Dirty Bertie

outside the school. Bertie bent down
and quickly stuffed the jumper under
his seat. He joined the queue, anxious
to get off. Once the coach drove away
he'd be home and dry, free at last! He
jumped down the steps and hurried to
the gates.

"OH, BERTIE!" sang a voice
behind him. "Aren't you forgetting
something?"

Bertie swung round.
His heart sunk.
Know-All Nick was
waving the dreaded
jumper in the air.

"Noooo!"
moaned Bertie.
Was he never going
to get rid of it!

CHAPTER 4

For the rest of the day Bertie put up with all the funny comments about his jumper.

"HA HA! Look at Bertie!"

"Did you knit that yourself?"

"Is it a jumper or a dress?"

Bertie tried everything to get rid of it. He left it in the cloakroom, the toilets

Dirty Bertie

and even in the lost property box. But the jumper always came back like a boomerang. Know-All Nick made it his personal mission to make sure he found it. In desperation, Bertie tried to throw the jumper into a tree, but he missed and it flopped down, landing on Miss Boot's head. At the end of the day Bertie plodded home with his friends.

"Cheer up, Bertie," said Eugene. "I bet everyone will have forgotten it by tomorrow."

"Not if my mum makes me wear it again," moaned Bertie. "It's so big I'll still be wearing it when I'm eighteen!"

"Hey, Bertie, catch!"

A ball whizzed past his head, bounced off a lamppost and shot over a fence.

Darren threw up his hands. "That's my super bouncy ball! Why didn't you catch it?" he grumbled.

"It's not my fault," replied Bertie. "I wasn't even looking!"

They peered over a tall wooden fence into a front garden. The ball lay in the middle of the lawn.

"We could climb over and get it," suggested Eugene.

"Darren could," said Bertie. "It's *his* ball."

"I'm not going! You're the one who lost it," argued Darren.

Bertie sighed and took off his coat.

Darren gave him a leg up and helped

him climb over the fence. Getting the
ball was the easy part – getting back
proved more difficult. Bertie had to
jump and hang on while trying to haul
himself up. Eventually he managed to get
one leg over the fence. That was when
something got caught.

"AAARGH! I'm stuck!" he wailed.

"Hurry up, I think someone's coming!"
warned Eugene.

Dirty Bertie

Bertie gave one last tug and managed to pull himself free. He jumped down, almost landing on top of Darren.

Eugene pointed. "Oh no, look what you've done!"

Bertie looked down. A thread of wool hung loose from the bottom of his jumper. It must have caught on the fence! He shrugged his shoulders. It was too late to do anything about it now.

Back home, Bertie walked in and dumped his coat on the floor. His mum was in the kitchen having tea with Gran.

"Here he is!" cried Gran. "And look, he's wearing his lovely new— Oh dear!"

She broke off. Mum raised a hand to her head.

Dirty Bertie

"What?" said Bertie. "What's wrong?"
Looking down, he saw that the
knitted jumper had shrunk. In fact most
of the bottom half was gone, leaving
only the lambs' jolly faces. A long thread
of wool led back down the hallway and
out of the door. It must have unravelled
on the way home!

"Oops! Sorry, Gran," mumbled Bertie.

Mum shook her head in despair.
"Really, how do you manage it, Bertie?
You only wore it for one day!"

One day was quite enough, thought
Bertie. He tried to look sorry but inside
he felt like dancing. Yahoo! He'd got
rid of it! He'd never have to wear the
knitted horror again!

"Oh well, these things happen," sighed
Gran. "Luckily for you I've just seen the
perfect thing in my magazine – a rainbow
jumper with darling little bunnies."

Bertie turned pale.

"Aww! I'm sure he'll love it," cooed
Mum. "What do you say to Gran,
Bertie?"

GOLD!

CHAPTER 1

Bertie and his friends were on the way back from their Saturday trip to the sweet shop.

"You won't believe what my dad's just bought," said Eugene.

"A speed boat," said Bertie.

"Even better than that," said Eugene. "A metal detector!"

Dirty Bertie

Bertie and Darren stared.

"A metal *detective*?" said Darren.

"No, a *detector*," repeated Eugene. "It's a machine which finds stuff buried in the ground."

"Like dead bodies, you mean?" said Bertie.

"No! Metal stuff like spoons or rings," explained Eugene. "If you're really lucky you might even find gold!"

"GOLD?" Bertie almost choked on his jelly snake.

"Well, obviously not all the time," admitted Eugene. "So far we've only found a sardine tin and an old dog tag. But my dad says a man once dug up treasure worth millions. It was sitting in a field for hundreds of years and nobody knew."

Bertie's eyes shone. This was fantastic! He'd always dreamed of finding buried treasure and here was his big chance!

"Well, what are we waiting for?" he cried.

"You think there's gold buried round here?" asked Darren.

"I don't see why not, there are loads of fields," replied Bertie. "And if we've got your detective machine we're bound to find it."

"It's not mine though, it's my dad's," Eugene reminded them. "And he doesn't like me using it without him."

"But we only need it for a few hours," said Bertie.

"Yes, and you don't have to tell him we borrowed it," said Darren.

"Hmm," said Eugene doubtfully. "Well, I suppose not."

They waited while Eugene ran home to fetch the metal detector. Bertie couldn't think why his parents hadn't bought their own machine. Didn't they *know* you could find actual GOLD buried in the ground?

Soon Eugene was back. The metal detector looked like a space-age walking stick. It had a metal ring at one end, and a screen with a dial.

Dirty Bertie

"That's it?" said Bertie.

"I thought it would be more like a giant digger," said Darren.

Eugene looked anxious. "I have to get it back by this afternoon," he warned. "If my dad finds out we've borrowed it, he'll go up the wall."

"That gives us plenty of time," said Bertie. "Let's try it in my back garden."

Bertie's mum was working at the kitchen table.

"Hello," she said. "And where are you three off to?"

"Just to play in the garden," answered Bertie. "We're hunting for buried treasure."

"Oh, I see," smiled Mum. "And what's

Dirty Bertie

that you've got, Eugene?"

"It's a metal detector – we're, er …
borrowing it from my dad," said Eugene.

"It'll show us if there's gold in the back
garden," explained Bertie.

Mum raised her eyebrows. "Well,
good luck with that," she said. "Just
make sure you don't tread on any of
my plants."

"We won't!" Bertie promised.

He hurried outside. Who cared about
a few droopy old plants? If they found
gold they'd be able to buy a palace with
its own garden, swimming pool and
even a helicopter pad!

CHAPTER 2

The treasure hunters decided to start on the back lawn.

"I should go first, because it's my garden," said Bertie.

"Yes, but it's my metal detector," argued Eugene.

"What about me? When do I get a turn?" grumbled Darren.

Dirty Bertie

In the end Eugene went first as he was the only one who knew how to make the metal detector work. Bertie thought it looked pretty simple – you just pointed it at the ground and if it beeped and went crazy you'd found gold.

Eugene clicked a button and moved the metal ring from side to side as the machine hummed and ticked.

"Anything?" asked Bertie.

"Give me a chance," said Eugene. "If it finds anything it makes a noise and the needle on the dial jumps about."

Bertie moved in closer, watching the needle for the faintest movement. They reached the bottom of the lawn without a beep from the machine then turned around.

"Let me try," said Bertie, grabbing it.

Dirty Bertie

"Maybe you're not doing it right."

"I am!" said Eugene. "You just have to give it time."

Bertie strode up the lawn, waving the detector around like a magic wand.

"You're doing it too fast!" cried Eugene. "You have to take it—"

BEEP! BEEP! BEEP!

Bertie stopped dead. The needle had shot up the dial. This was it! They'd found gold!

"Quick, get a spade!" he cried.

Darren found a spade in the shed and started to dig.

"WAIT!" shouted Bertie.

He bent down and picked something out of the mud. It was a dirty toy car missing a wheel.

Dirty Bertie

"I wondered where that had got to," said Bertie.

"Huh! So much for finding gold!" sighed Darren.

"I told you it picks up anything that's metal," said Eugene. "You're not going to find gold coins every single time."

For the next half an hour, they combed the lawn from top to bottom. At last they sat down to inspect their finds. There was a swimming badge, a rusty screw, a toy car and a penny. It wasn't exactly the treasure Bertie had in mind.

Dirty Bertie

"Maybe we're not looking in the right place," he sighed.

"My dad says it's all about knowing where to search," agreed Eugene. "For instance, in the old days the Romans probably lived around here."

"What? In Bertie's house?" said Darren.

"No! But sometimes people find bits of Roman pottery in their gardens," said Eugene. "I've seen them in Pudsley museum."

"Well, if they've found pottery, I bet there's gold buried somewhere," said Bertie.

He'd been hoping for pirate treasure but Roman gold was even better! There might be gold cups, helmets, swords and daggers studded with jewels. Maybe they'd find a Roman money box stuffed with gold coins! Think how much that would be worth – millions or possibly billions.

"I know, let's look in the park," Bertie suggested.

"Why the park?" asked Eugene.

"Why not? The Romans must have had parks," Bertie argued.

"Yes, but thousands of years ago it probably wasn't a park," Eugene pointed out. "It could have been the Roman baths!"

"Even better," said Bertie. "People are always leaving stuff at the baths."

"Hang on, though," said Darren. "You can't go digging up the park."

"Why not?" asked Bertie. "It's only grass. Who's going to care about a few little holes?"

Dirty Bertie

Speaking of holes, he noticed that the
back lawn had quite a few. Small piles
of earth lay heaped everywhere you
looked. Mum wasn't going to be too
pleased about that. Maybe a trip to the
park was a good idea!

CHAPTER 3

The park was busy with people. Whiffer had tagged along, despite Bertie ordering him to go home. He was now bounding around getting in everyone's way. The treasure hunters looked around.

"This is no good," said Eugene. "We'll never find anything with all these people."

Dirty Bertie

"HEY YOU!"

A man in uniform was marching towards them. Bertie groaned. Mr Monk lived on his street and was always complaining. Now he was a park-keeper he had a lot more to complain about, such as litter, dog poo and children enjoying themselves.

"Is that your dog?" he demanded. "I've just seen him digging in the sandpit."

"Sorry, Mr Monk," mumbled Bertie.

The park-keeper folded his arms. "And what are you three up to?"

"Nothing," replied Bertie.

Mr Monk pointed a finger. "Is that a metal detector?"

"Um, yes ... it's my dad's. We're borrowing it," admitted Eugene.

Dirty Bertie

"Humph," said Mr Monk. "Well, you can't use it here. Metal detectors aren't allowed in the park."

"We're not using it," explained Bertie. "We're just looking after it."

"Is that right?" frowned Mr Monk. "Well, you better behave. I've got my eye on you and don't forget it."

He stomped off back to his weeding.

"Maybe we should look somewhere else," suggested Eugene.

"I don't see why," said Bertie. "It's our park as much as his."

"Yes, but you heard him, metal detectors aren't allowed," said Darren. "We can't go digging up the grass."

"We're not digging up anything," said Bertie. "We're just going for a little walk. Come on."

They walked on until they were out of sight. Bertie switched on the metal detector and it hummed into life.

The park turned out to be the perfect place to find treasure — but only if you wanted bottle caps, ring pulls or drink cans. After an hour of poking around among the trees, Darren and Eugene had had enough.

"Let's go home," moaned Darren. "We're never going to find any gold."

"At least we found 2p, it's better than nothing," said Eugene.

But Bertie wasn't beaten yet. If someone had found Roman gold in a field why couldn't they find it in the park?

"One last try," he begged. "We haven't looked over there yet."

He pointed to a flower bed full of Mr Monk's prize roses.

"Bertie! We can't!" said Eugene. "What if Mr Monk comes back?"

Bertie looked around. "He's not here," he said. "He's probably gone home for lunch. Anyway it'll only take a minute!"

They crept in among the rose bushes.

Dirty Bertie

"POOH! It stinks!" cried Darren, stepping in some compost.

"Hurry up, Bertie, before he comes," said Eugene.

Bertie swept the metal detector over the earth. Nothing. He walked forward...

BEEP! BEEP! BEEP!

"I've got something!" he cried.

The needle on the dial was going crazy. Bertie got down on his hands and knees, digging with the spade they'd brought. It didn't take long before he found it – a single coin shining silver in the dirt.

"Look!" cried Bertie, grabbing it. This was it – they'd struck gold – or silver at least.

They crowded round to examine the coin. It looked old, although it was hard to tell because it was covered in dirt.

"Let's take it back to your house and clean it up," suggested Eugene.

Just then Whiffer came racing up and barked. Bertie looked round. Mr Monk was charging down the path like an angry bull.

"OI! GET AWAY FROM MY ROSES!" he roared.

"Uh-oh," said Bertie. Faced with a hopping-mad Mr Monk there was only one thing to do – run for their lives.

CHAPTER 4

On Bertie's road, they stopped to get
their breath back. Mr Monk had chased
them to the park gates but seemed to
have given up.

"That was terrible!" panted Eugene.
"What if he tells our parents?"

"Never mind that," said Darren.
"Have you still got the coin, Bertie?"

Dirty Bertie

Bertie pulled it from his pocket and wiped it on his trousers.

It smelled pongy but it wasn't like any coin he'd seen before. It was silver with writing around the edge.

"I bet you it's Roman," said Bertie. "It's even got the king's head on it."

"The Romans had emperors," Eugene pointed out.

"Well, the emperor's head, then. It must be worth loads," said Bertie. "Maybe two or three million."

Wait till they heard about this at school, he thought. Miss Boot would be amazed.

Dirty Bertie

She'd probably ask him to give a talk about the Romans in assembly. They'd get their picture in all the papers. They'd probably get their own TV show. Bertie tossed the coin high into the air…

OOOPS! The coin slipped through his fingers, hit the pavement and rolled away. It vanished down a drain with a plop!

Dirty Bertie

There was a stunned silence.

"You idiot, Bertie!" groaned Darren. "What did you do that for?"

"I didn't mean to," cried Bertie. "I meant to catch it!"

He got down on his hands and knees and peered into the drain. He could see the coin, shining silver among the mucky gunk and leaves. He tried to wriggle his hand through the bars of the drain but the gap was too narrow.

"I don't believe it," grumbled Darren. "At last we find a Roman coin and you chuck it away!"

"It was an accident!" said Bertie. "There must be some way to get it back."

"There is one thing we could try," said Eugene. "Wait here!"

Dirty Bertie

Ten minutes later, Bertie and Darren
watched as Eugene lowered a piece of
string down into the drain. Tied to the
end was a super strong magnet.
Eugene fished around. It took
a few attempts but finally he
pulled the string slowly back
up. The silver coin was stuck
to the magnet, caked in mud.
Bertie grabbed it before it
fell. Yes! They were back in
business.

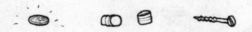

In the kitchen, Bertie's mum was making
lunch.

"You'll never guess what we found!"
cried Bertie, running in.

"Don't tell me – buried treasure,"

said Mum.

"Yes! A Roman coin!" said Bertie, holding it up. "It's real silver and millions of years old!"

Mum took it from him. "A Roman coin, hmm? Let's have a look at it," she said.

Going over to the sink, she washed off all the mud and held the coin up to the light.

"Ah, that's interesting," she said. "I wonder where it came from."

Dirty Bertie

"Is it Roman?" asked Bertie hopefully.

"Hardly," laughed Mum. "It's Canadian. Look, it says there, fifty cents."

"WHAT?" cried Bertie.

After all they'd been through to rescue the coin, it turned out it wasn't Roman at all! The treasure hunters looked at each other. Bertie's shoulders drooped.

"You mean it's not worth millions?" he asked.

"I doubt it," said Mum. "Maybe around 10p. Still, I'll look after it while you finish your jobs."

"Jobs?" said Bertie. "What jobs?"

Mum steered him to the window.

"It looks like someone dug up half the lawn," she said. "I'd like all those holes filled in, please. Now."

Dirty Bertie

Bertie rolled his eyes. It was the last time they borrowed a metal detector. The only thing they'd found all day was heaps of trouble!

For Daniel Barrie ~ D R

For Liz and Stephen – Our Friends in
the North ~ A M

Contents

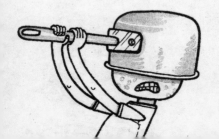

CHAPTER 1

"Go on," said Darren. "I dare you. Before he comes back."

Bertie looked at the hammer. It belonged to Mr Grouch, the demon caretaker. Bertie and Darren were helping him with the scenery for the school play. So far they had done nothing but stand around listening to the caretaker grumble.

Dirty Bertie

But Mr Grouch wasn't around right now. He'd gone off to fetch more nails, leaving his hammer lying on the stage.

"Why don't you do it?" asked Bertie.

"I dared you first," said Darren.

"I dare you back," said Bertie.

"I double dare you no returns," said Darren.

Bertie looked around. He never refused a dare, not even the time Darren dared him to lock Mr Weakly in the store cupboard. And this was just one little tap with a hammer. What harm could it do? A nail was sticking up practically begging to be hit. Bertie picked up the hammer and took a swing.

"Watch what you're doing!" cried Darren, ducking out of the way.

Dirty Bertie

"Well, stand back then," said Bertie.
"I need room."

He glanced round, checking that no
one was about. All clear.

DINK! He tapped the nail on the head.

Darren rolled his eyes. "Not like that!
Give it a proper whack."

Dirty Bertie

Bertie held the nail between his finger
and thumb. He swung the hammer back
and brought it down.

THUNK!

"YOWWWWW!" he
wailed, dropping the hammer.
"What did you do?" said
Darren.

"I HIT MY
THUMB! ARGH!
OWW!" Bertie hopped
around like a frog on a dance floor.

"SHHH!" hissed Darren. "Someone
will hear you!"

Bertie was in too much pain to care.
"OWW! OWW! OWW!" he howled.

Footsteps came thudding down the
corridor. Mr Grouch burst into the hall,
followed by Miss Boot.

Dirty Bertie

"WHAT IS GOING ON?" yelled Miss Boot.

"Nothing, Miss," said Darren.

"ARGH! OHHHH!" cried Bertie, doubled over in pain.

Mr Grouch spotted the hammer on the floor.

"Have you been playing with this?" he growled, picking it up.

Darren shook his head. "No," he said. "*I* haven't!"

Miss Boot turned on Bertie. "Did you touch this hammer?"

"I was only trying to help!" moaned Bertie.

"I knew it!" cried Mr Grouch. "I turn my back for two seconds and this is what happens. That boy is a menace. He should be expelled!"

Dirty Bertie

"Yes, thank you, Mr Grouch," said Miss
Boot. "I will deal with this."

"OWW! OWW!" wailed Bertie.
"I think it's broken!"

"Don't make such a fuss!" snapped
Miss Boot. "Let me see."

Dirty Bertie

Bertie let go of his thumb and held it out for inspection. Yikes! It had turned purple and swollen up like a balloon! "I don't feel very well," he said, going pale.

Miss Boot took charge. "Darren, take him to Miss Skinner's office," she ordered. "And Bertie, don't think you've heard the last of this, I shall be speaking to your parents."

Bertie sat outside Miss Skinner's office nursing his injured thumb. It was wrapped in a wet paper towel. He couldn't believe the way everyone was remaining so calm. Why hadn't they called an ambulance? For all they knew he could be dying!

Dirty Bertie

The door flew open and his mum hurried in.

"Bertie, are you all right?" she cried.

Bertie shook his head weakly and held up his hand.

"I think it's broken!" he moaned.

"Your hand?"

"My thumb."

"Well, what happened?"

"It wasn't my fault," said Bertie. "I was trying to help. The hammer slipped."

"Hammer!" shrieked Mum. "What on earth were you doing with a hammer?"

"Hammering," replied Bertie.

"Well next time, *don't.* Hammers are dangerous," said Mum. "Let me see."

Bertie gingerly unwrapped the soggy paper towel. His thumb was still swollen.

Mum stared. "Is that it?" she said.
"I thought it was serious!"

"It hurts!" said Bertie. "It's probably
broken!"

"So you keep saying," sighed Mum.
"Well, we'd better get it checked out.
Let's get you to hospital."

CHAPTER 2

Later that afternoon, Bertie sat in the
hospital waiting room. It was packed
with people. Bertie stared at a small girl
with her foot in plaster. Beside her was
a man in a neck collar and a boy with
a saucepan jammed on his head. You
got all kinds of people in hospitals.
Bertie checked his thumb again to see

if it had got any bigger. It hadn't.

He looked at the clock. They had been waiting for hours and he hadn't eaten since lunch. His stomach gurgled. If they waited much longer he might pass out with hunger. Tempting smells drifted across from the snack bar.

"Mum, can I get some crisps?" asked Bertie.

"No," said Mum. "I thought you were in agony."

"I AM," said Bertie. "But crisps might take my mind off it."

Mum gave him a weary look. "You're not having crisps now," she said.

Bertie sighed. "How about a doughnut, then?"

"NO, Bertie!" snapped Mum. "Just sit quietly and wait for the doctor."

Dirty Bertie

Bertie slumped in his seat. Talking about food only made him hungrier. Maybe he could just investigate what the snack bar had to offer? He got up.

"Where are you going?" asked Mum, lowering her magazine.

"Nowhere! Just to have a look," pleaded Bertie.

"Well, stay where I can keep an eye on you," said Mum.

There was a queue of people at the counter. Bertie hung around for a while, hoping someone might take pity on a starving boy. No one did. On a nearby table he noticed a bowl containing small packets of mayonnaise, tomato ketchup and mustard. Bertie slipped a couple of them into his pocket as emergency supplies for later. He looked up and

Dirty Bertie

found a boy with his arm in a sling watching him.

"What happened to you?" asked Bertie.

The boy shrugged. "Hit a lamp post."

"With your arm?" said Bertie.

"No, on my bike," said the boy.

"I hit my thumb with a hammer," said Bertie, proudly. He unwound the paper towel to show off his swollen thumb.

Dirty Bertie

The boy shrugged. "Huh! That's nothing," he scoffed. "I'm always in hospital. This is the second time I broke my arm. Broke my collar bone too."

"Wow!" said Bertie, impressed. The only thing he'd ever broken was the upstairs toilet.

The boy lowered his voice. "They don't let you stay unless it's serious," he said.

"Stay where?" said Bertie.

"On the children's ward." The boy gave him a pitying look. "Haven't you ever been in hospital?"

Bertie shook his head.

"You don't know what you're missing!" said the boy. "You don't have to do nothing — just lie in bed all day, watching TV. No going to school — nothing."

Bertie gawped at the boy. Staying in

hospital sounded like paradise! Much better than listening to Miss Boot droning on for hours. Maybe the hospital would keep him in for a few days, or even a week? He noticed his mum beckoning him to sit down.

"Better go," he said.

The boy nodded. "Okay. Maybe catch you on the children's ward later?"

"I'll be there," said Bertie.

He went back to his seat.

"Who was that?" asked Mum.

"Don't know," replied Bertie. "We just got talking. Mum, how long do you think I'll have to stay in hospital?"

Mum laughed. "Bertie, you've only bruised your thumb!"

"It might be broken," Bertie reminded her.

Dirty Bertie

Mum shook her head. "If it was, you'd be in agony."

"I *am* in agony!" said Bertie. "I'm just not making a fuss!"

"You fooled me," said Mum. "In any case, they'll probably just give you a plaster and send you home."

Bertie stared. Send him home with a plaster? They couldn't do that! What about missing school?

CHAPTER 3

"Bertie BURNS?" called a loud voice. Bertie looked up. A red-haired nurse with a clipboard was looking round the waiting room. Her badge said "Nurse Nettles".

"Over here!" said Mum, standing up.

"Follow me, would you please?" said the nurse.

Bertie and Mum followed her down the corridor and into a cubicle with a bed, a table and a couple of plastic chairs. The nurse drew the curtain across and looked briskly at Bertie.

"Well, young man, what have you been up to?" she said.

"Nothing," frowned Bertie. "I hurt my thumb."

"He hit it with a hammer," explained Mum.

"Not on purpose," said Bertie. The way everyone talked you'd think he had.

Nurse Nettles wrote something on a form. "Let's have a look at it then, shall we?" she said.

Bertie winced as Nurse Nettles unwound the paper towel. The thumb was still purple, though not quite as

Dirty Bertie

swollen as Bertie remembered.

"Mmm, yes, I see," said Nurse Nettles. "Try and move it for me."

Bertie waggled his thumb gingerly.

"OUCH!" he yelled.

"Now bend it back."

Bertie bent it back.

"ARGHH!"

"Well?" asked Mum. "Is it serious?"

Nurse Nettles smiled. "I don't think so. Badly bruised, that's all."

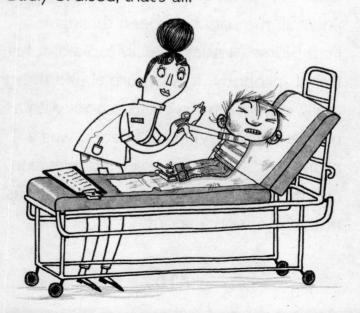

Dirty Bertie

"BRUISED?" cried Bertie. "Not broken?"

"Not broken," said Nurse Nettles. "But we'll get Dr Dose to examine you."

This was more like it.

"Does that mean I have to stay in hospital?" asked Bertie.

Nurse Nettles laughed. "No, don't worry, you'll be going home in no time."

She went off to find the doctor.

Bertie slumped back on the bed. Bruised? Was that all? It was so unfair! After all the pain he'd been through! Had Nurse Nettles actually looked at his thumb properly? It was purple! Did they really expect him to go to school with a purple thumb? What he needed was a proper rest – rest and unlimited television.

"You see?" said Mum. "I told you it was nothing to worry about."

Dirty Bertie

Bertie scowled. If only his thumb was hanging off, spurting fountains of blood everywhere. If only it had gone bad and was dripping with yellow pus. Wait a moment… Bertie felt in his pocket. He still had the little packets he'd got from the snack bar. Mustard was yellow. All he needed was a minute to himself, before the doctor came.

He jumped to his feet. "I need the toilet!" he said.

"What? Now?" said Mum. "Can't you wait?"

"No!" said Bertie. "Won't be a minute." He dashed off.

CHAPTER 4

By the time Bertie got back, Dr Dose had arrived and was talking to his mum and Nurse Nettles.

"Right then," said Dr Dose, rubbing his hands. "Let's have a look at this thumb, shall we?"

Bertie nodded weakly and held it up for him to see.

Dirty Bertie

"Good heavens!" said Nurse Nettles.
Bertie's thumb had turned a funny
colour. Globs of yellow oozed and
dripped on to the floor.

"What happened?" cried Mum.

"I don't know!" groaned Bertie. "I think
it's infected!"

Dr Dose pushed his glasses up his
nose. "It does look odd. Let me see."

He peered closely at the thumb.
"Cotton wool, please, nurse," he said.

Dirty Bertie

He dabbed at the messy thumb and sniffed the cotton wool.

"Ah," he said. "Just as I thought. Mustarditis."

Nurse Nettles giggled.

Bertie looked up at them. "Is that bad?"

"Very bad," said Doctor Dose.

"Mustarditis?" repeated Mum.

Dr Dose gave her a wink. "Perhaps you could wait outside while I talk to Bertie."

"Yes, I think *someone* should," said Mum.

Bertie sat on the bed. His brilliant trick had fooled everyone. *Children's ward, here I come!* he thought. *A whole week off school!*

"Will I have to stay in hospital?" he asked, feebly.

"For a while," said Dr Dose. "After the operation."

Dirty Bertie

Bertie gasped. Operation? No one had said anything about an operation!

"W-what?" he mumbled.

"Well, your thumb's turned yellow," said Dr Dose. "Very bad, mustarditis. The only thing is to operate right away. Wouldn't you agree, Nurse Nettles?"

Nurse Nettles nodded, trying not to laugh.

Bertie stared at them. All he wanted was a few days off school – not this! He imagined the operating theatre. There would be an injection – with a long needle. Doctors in masks. What if they decided his thumb couldn't be saved? What if they chopped it off? He needed his thumb to beat Darren at Mega Monster Racing!

Dirty Bertie

Dr Dose put something on. It was a green mask.

"Right," he said brightly. "Shall we get started?"

"NOOO!" cried Bertie, leaping off the bed.

He rushed through the curtains, hurrying past his mum, who was waiting outside.

Dirty Bertie

"HELP! SAVE ME!" he gasped. "Don't let them get me!"

"I thought your thumb was agony," said Mum.

"No!" said Bertie. "Look, it's better!" He licked his thumb. "It was only mustard."

Dr Dose and Nurse Nettles peered through the curtains. They were laughing and wiping their eyes. Bertie gaped. The truth dawned on him. There was no operation – it was all a joke.

"So," said Mum. "Mustard, eh?"

"Um, yes," said Bertie. "I must have somehow got a bit on my thumb."

"Really? I wonder how that could have happened," said Mum dryly.

"Never mind," said Nurse Nettles brightly. "Let's find you a plaster, shall we?"

Dirty Bertie

Bertie went back to sit on the bed.
A plaster – after all he'd been through!
He'd told Darren his thumb was broken
and by now the story would be all
round school. No one was going to be
very impressed if he came back wearing
a stupid little plaster.

Nurse Nettles looked in a drawer.
She held out a plaster the size of a
postage stamp. Bertie looked at her.

"Actually," he said, "you don't have
something a bit bigger, do you?"

Dirty Bertie

BOTTOM!

CHAPTER 1

"LAST ONE CHANGED IS A
STINKER!" shouted Darren.

Bertie banged into the cubicle and
dumped his bag on the seat. It was Friday
– swimming day. He stripped off his
clothes, dropping them in a messy heap.
Then he picked up his bag and emptied
it out. Goggles, towel, shower gel…

Dirty Bertie

Wait a minute, where were his swimming trunks? His heart missed a beat. He picked up his towel and shook it out. Nothing! He searched the bottom of his bag. Empty! Surely he hadn't … he couldn't have left his swimming trunks at home? Miss Boot would go up the wall!

He wrapped a towel round his waist and climbed on to the seat.

"Psssst! Eugene!" he hissed, peering into the next cubicle.

"What?" Eugene blinked at him through his goggles.

"I forgot my trunks!" said Bertie.

"You're joking!" said Eugene.

Darren's head popped up from the next cubicle along. "What's going on?"

"Bertie's forgotten his trunks," explained Eugene.

Dirty Bertie

"You haven't!"

"I HAVE!" groaned Bertie. "You've got to help! Miss Boot will kill me!"

His friends nodded grimly. A few weeks ago Trevor had forgotten his towel. Miss Boot had made him do twenty laps of the changing room to dry off.

"What am I going to do?" moaned Bertie.

Darren shrugged. "You'll just have to wear your pants."

Dirty Bertie

Bertie gave him a look. "I can't swim in my pants!" he said. His pants had holes in them and, besides, they looked like … well, like pants. He turned to Eugene.

"Didn't you bring a spare pair?"

"Why would I do that?" asked Eugene.

"So I can borrow them, of course!"

Eugene shook his head.

"Darren, what about you?" pleaded Bertie.

"Sorry, can't help," said Darren.

Bertie gave a heavy sigh. He was sunk.

There was a loud bang on the changing-room door.

"ONE MINUTE! GET A MOVE ON!" bellowed Miss Boot.

"Sorry, Bertie, we better go," said Eugene. "You know how mad she gets if you're late."

Dirty Bertie

"Yeah," said Darren. "Good luck!"

The two of them hurried out, leaving Bertie alone. He slumped on the seat in despair. Suddenly, an ugly face appeared in the gap under the door. It was Know-All Nick, the last person on earth he wanted to see.

Dirty Bertie

"Oh dear, Bertie, forgotten your swimming trunks?" he jeered. "Wait till Miss Boot finds out!" He disappeared, sniggering to himself.

Bertie sank back against the wall. Maybe if he just stayed here, he wouldn't be missed and the swimming lesson would go ahead without him. Afterwards he could wet his hair under the tap and slip on to the coach.

WHAM! The changing-room door flew open. Footsteps thudded down the corridor.

"Bertie! WHERE ARE YOU?" boomed Miss Boot. "Come out of there!"

"I can't!" moaned Bertie. "I haven't got any trunks!"

Miss Boot raised her eyes to heaven. Why did it always have to be Bertie?

"Open this door!" she ordered.

Bertie slid back the lock and peeped out, holding the towel round his waist.

"Couldn't I just sit and watch?" he pleaded.

"Certainly not!" snapped Miss Boot. "You'll just have to borrow some trunks."

Dirty Bertie

"I've tried!" said Bertie. "No one's got any."

"Then go to Reception and ask them to lend you a pair," said Miss Boot. "And get a move on. Everyone's waiting!"

Bertie nodded and shuffled past Miss Boot. As he reached the door, he trod on his towel.

"Bertie!" Miss Boot groaned and covered her eyes.

CHAPTER 2

Bertie stood in Reception. The woman
behind the desk was talking on the phone.

"Yes? Can I help you?" she said,
putting it down at last.

"Um ... yes," said Bertie, "I don't have
any swimming trunks."

"Oh dear!" said the woman. "Didn't
you bring them?"

Dirty Bertie

"I forgot," said Bertie. "They're probably at home – in my pants drawer."

"Well, you're not allowed in the pool without a costume, it's against the rules," said the woman.

"I know," said Bertie. "But Miss Boot said you might have some swimming trunks I could borrow."

"I see," sighed the woman. She looked at her coffee, which was getting cold. "Wait there," she said. "I'll see what I can do."

Bertie waited. It was embarrassing standing in the middle of Reception, wearing only a towel. A small girl over by the drinks machine was staring at him. Finally, the woman came back carrying a large green box, marked "Lost Property". She put it down on the floor.

Dirty Bertie

"Here we are," she said. "There's not much, but take your pick."

Bertie peered inside. The box contained a pair of orange water wings, a swimming cap, a spotty bikini and a single pair of swimming trunks. Bertie fished them out. They were silver Speedos, hardly bigger than a paper tissue.

"Is this all there is?" he gasped.

The woman sniffed. "Looks like it."

"But haven't you got anything else? Like normal swimming shorts?"

The woman glared. "We're not a shop!" she snapped. "Do you want them or not?"

Bertie nodded miserably. He had no choice. He shuffled back to the changing room, holding the trunks as if they were riddled with fleas. Wait till his friends saw him! He was going to be the laughing stock of the whole class.

He locked himself inside the cubicle and pulled on the silver trunks. They were so old that the elastic had gone, and no matter how tightly he tied them, they wouldn't stay up! He looked down in horror. There was no way he could wear these.

Dirty Bertie

Someone thumped on the door. "Bertie! HURRY UP!" thundered Miss Boot. "WE'RE WAITING FOR YOU!"

Bertie groaned. He opened the cubicle door and slunk out.

Miss Boot stared. "What on earth are those?" she said.

"Swimming trunks," wailed Bertie. "It's all they had!"

Dirty Bertie

"Very well, they'll have to do," said Miss Boot. "Pull them up and let's go."

The class were sitting by the side of the pool, with their feet in the water. Miss Crawl leaned against the rail, impatient to get started. She was a tall, thin woman who had once been Junior Backstroke Champion.

Everyone looked round as Bertie appeared. He ducked behind Miss Boot, but it was too late. Know-All Nick had seen him.

"HA HA! LOOK AT Bertie!" he hooted.

"Nice trunks, Bertie!" giggled Donna.

"Are they your grandad's?" screeched Trevor.

Bertie glared at them and plodded over to join the end of the line.

Dirty Bertie

"Oh, Bertie," sang Nick. "We can see your bottom!"

Bertie went bright red and hitched up the saggy Speedos. This was terrible! How was he going to get through an entire swimming lesson without dying of embarrassment?

CHAPTER 3

Bertie clung to the side of the pool, shivering with cold. The lesson had only been going half an hour, but it felt like a lifetime. He had hardly dared leave the side for fear of losing his trunks.

Know-All Nick zoomed past, splashing him in the face.

"BERTIE!" bellowed a voice.

Dirty Bertie

Uh oh, Miss Boot had spotted him.

"What are you doing?" she called.
"Miss Crawl, why isn't Bertie joining in?"

"Good question," said Miss Crawl.
"Bertie, what do you think you're doing?"

"Nothing," said Bertie.

"Well, get away from the side. I said four lengths' breaststroke!"

"I can't!" wailed Bertie.

"Why not?"

"My trunks keep falling down!"

"No feeble excuses!" snapped Miss Crawl. "Get swimming!"

Bertie groaned. He pushed off and swam after the rest of the class. ARGHH! The saggy Speedos were falling down again! He could feel them slipping towards his knees. He tried swimming with one hand while holding on to the stupid trunks with the other. It was hard work. He kept sinking and glugging great gulps of water.

"Come on, Bertie, keep up!" shouted Darren, speeding past.

At last he made it to the far end and hung on to the rail, gasping for breath. Know-All Nick climbed out by the steps.

Dirty Bertie

He hurried over to Miss Crawl,
dripping wet.

"Miss! OOOH! OOH! I need the
toilet!" he whimpered.

Miss Crawl scowled. "Can't you hang
on?"

"No! I've got to goooo!" cried Nick,
jiggling from foot to foot.

"Oh, very well!" sighed Miss Crawl. "Hurry up!"

Bertie watched Nick patter off towards the changing room. Suddenly, he was struck by an idea. It was so simple it was genius. But he'd have to move fast or it would be too late. Bertie swam to the steps and climbed out.

"What now?" said Miss Crawl.

"Miss! I need the toilet, Miss!" pleaded Bertie.

"Not you as well? You'll just have to wait till the lesson is over."

"But I can't!" said Bertie, dancing up and down. "I have to go! NOW!"

Miss Crawl sighed heavily. "Go on then. Make it quick!"

Dirty Bertie

Bertie pushed open the changing-room door. There was no one about. He stole over to the boys' toilets. He could hear Know-All Nick humming to himself in one of the cubicles. Bertie tiptoed over. He got down on his hands and knees to peer under the door. There were Nick's two white feet dangling in mid-air, with his red swimming trunks round his ankles.

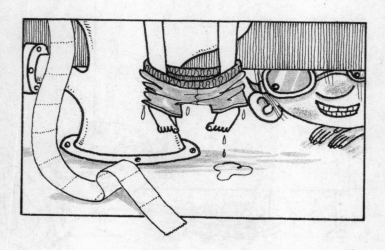

"Hmm hmm hmm!" Nick hummed to himself.

Slowly, silently, Bertie reached his hand under the door.

SNATCH!

He grabbed the red swimming trunks and yanked them off.

"ARGHHH!" cried Nick, overbalancing and falling off the toilet.

Dirty Bertie

"HEY! GIVE THEM BACK!" he howled.
"THEY'RE MINE!"

"Sorry, Nickerless!" replied Bertie.
"I need them."

Nick banged on the door. "I'll tell!"
he yelled. "You give them back, Bertie,
or I'll tell!"

There was no reply.

Cautiously, Know-All Nick unlocked
the door and came out. Bertie had
vanished. All that remained was a soggy
pair of Speedos lying on the floor.

CHAPTER 4

Back in the pool, Bertie joined the rest of the class.

PEEP! Miss Crawl blew her whistle. "Everyone out! Line up by the side!"

Eugene climbed out after Bertie. "Where did you get those trunks?" he asked, in surprise. "I thought yours were teeny-weeny."

Bertie grinned. "I'll tell you later."

"Right," said Miss Crawl. "I want you all to try the standing dive we did last week."

"Just a minute!" Miss Boot had been counting heads. "We're missing someone," she said. "Where is Nicholas?"

Miss Crawl frowned. "He went to the toilet, but that was ages ago."

Miss Boot marched over to the boys' changing room. She pounded on the door. THUMP! THUMP!

"Nicholas? Are you in there?"

No answer.

"NICHOLAS! Come out!"

"I CAN'T!" wailed a voice.

"Nonsense! What's the matter with you?" barked Miss Boot.

"I haven't got any trunks!"

"Don't be ridiculous, you were

wearing them earlier. Come out this instant!"

"Please don't make me!" snivelled Nick.

But Miss Boot was not a patient woman. "If you're not out in ten seconds I shall come in and drag you out," she warned.

The door opened slowly and Know-All Nick shuffled out. He was covering

Dirty Bertie

himself with a small yellow towel.

"Line up then!" ordered Miss Boot.

"But Miss, Bertie's—"

"Line up, I said! You're keeping everyone waiting!"

Know-All Nick gulped. He drooped over to join the line and put down his towel. He was wearing the saggy silver Speedos.

"HA HA!" hooted Bertie.

"Hee hee! Nice trunks, Nick!" giggled Darren.

"QUIET!" bawled Miss Crawl. "On my whistle, you will all dive in. Arms out, knees bent, heads down."

PEEP!

SPLASH! SPLOOSH! The class flopped into the pool one by one. Bertie bobbed to the surface and wiped his eyes. Something was floating on top of the water. A pair of silver swimming trunks. Bertie fished them out and waved them in the air.

"OH, NICKERLESS!" he cried. "DID YOU LOSE SOMETHING?"

Dirty Bertie

BRAINIAC!

SWOTTER
18

PUDSLEY
01

CHAPTER 1

It was Tuesday morning. Miss Boot put away the register and took out a letter.

"I have some good news for you," she said. "In two weeks' time it's the Junior Quiz Challenge and we will be entering a team."

The class turned pale. Bertie groaned. Of all the horrible tortures teachers had invented, the worst was the Junior Quiz Challenge. Four children forced on to a stage and made to answer endless *impossible* questions: What is the capital of Belgium? How many minutes in a fortnight? Can you spell "ignoramus"?

Every year Pudsley Junior entered a quiz team and every year they came bottom. Last time they'd scored a grand total of two and a half points – a record low in the history of the competition. A picture of the team had appeared in the *Pudsley Post* under the headline: "QUIZ FLOPS COME BOTTOM OF THE CLASS!"

Miss Boot had been furious. Miss Skinner said they'd brought shame on the whole school.

Bertie slid down in his chair. There was

no way he wanted to be on the team.
He'd rather dance down the high street
dressed as a fairy. But wait a second, why
did he need to worry? Miss Boot never
picked him for anything.

"Hands up," said Miss Boot, "who'd like
to be on the quiz team?"

Only one hand went up. It belonged
to Know-All Nick. *Trust smarty-pants Nick
to volunteer*, thought Bertie.

"Nicholas!" beamed Miss Boot.
"Marvellous! I knew you
would set an example."

Nick's head swelled
even larger than usual.

Dirty Bertie

"Who else? What about you, Donna?" asked Miss Boot.

"Umm…" said Donna.

"Excellent!" said Miss Boot. "And Eugene, I'm sure you'd be good!"

"Er … ah … mmm," mumbled Eugene.

"Splendid! That's three then," said Miss Boot. "So we just need one more to complete the team." Her gaze swept over the rows of faces. The class shrank back, desperate to avoid her eye. Darren raised his hand.

"What about Bertie, Miss?" he asked.

Bertie spun round. "Me? Are you mad?" He glared at Darren. Then he remembered. Yesterday he had put superglue on Darren's chair and Darren had vowed to get his revenge.

Miss Boot frowned. "I don't think so,"

Dirty Bertie

she said. "We need bright, clever children and Bertie is … well, his talents lie in other areas." This was true, thought Bertie. He was the class burping champion and he did a brilliant impression of Miss Boot.

"But, Miss, Bertie is brilliant at quizzes," claimed Darren, grinning at Bertie.

"NO I'M NOT!" cried Bertie.

"You are!" lied Darren. "You've always got your head in a quiz book."

"Thank you, Darren, I'll bear that in mind," said Miss Boot. She turned back to the class. "One more volunteer," she said. "Who'd like to represent our school? Royston?"

Royston shook his head.

"Nisha?"

Nisha hid behind Donna.

"Kylie?"

Kylie looked as if she might be sick.

Dirty Bertie

Miss Boot sighed heavily. "Very well then, Bertie, you're on the team."

"But, Miss…!" moaned Bertie.

"No need to thank me," said Miss Boot. "Just remember, I am giving you a chance, Bertie. Last year's team did not make their school proud. But this year will be different, because you will be prepared. And when the time comes, I expect you to win — is that clear?"

The quiz team nodded their heads gloomily. Bertie glared at Darren. This was so unfair!

CHAPTER 2

DRRRRRING! The bell went for lunchtime. Bertie headed for the door.

"Bertie!" called Know-All Nick. "Quiz team meeting!"

Bertie rolled his eyes and flopped into a chair beside Eugene. Who wanted to be stuck inside listening to Nick, when you could be outside playing?

Dirty Bertie

"Now," said Nick, "Miss Boot told me to choose a team captain. I think we all know who it should be."

"Who?" said Donna.

"Well, me, obviously," said Nick.

"Why you?"

"Because I'm the cleverest," boasted Nick.

"The ugliest, you mean," muttered Bertie.

Nick ignored him. "Practice sessions will be every lunchtime, starting today."

"*Every* lunchtime?" groaned Eugene. "How can we practise for a quiz?"

"By answering test questions, of course," said Nick. "Miss Boot lent me this." He reached into his bag and brought out *The Bumper Book of Quiz Fun*.

Dirty Bertie

"Right, I'll be quiz master," he said.

"And who's testing you?" asked Donna.

"No one, because I'm captain and I've got the book," said Nick. "Anyway, I don't need the practice. Bertie, you can go first because you're the most stupid. Eugene, you time him. You've got one minute."

Eugene set the timer on his watch.

Dirty Bertie

"Donna, you keep the score. Ready?" said Nick, settling on a page in the book. "Go…! Hades was the god of what?"

"Never heard of him," said Bertie.

"He's a Greek god, stupid, like Zeus and Mars."

"Isn't that a chocolate bar?" said Bertie.

"What?"

"Mars."

"Yes! No! I'm asking the questions!" snapped Nick, getting muddled.

"Well, what's the good of asking me stuff I don't know?" grumbled Bertie. "Why don't you try asking me something I do know?"

Nick sighed. "Next question…"

"Time's up!" shouted Eugene.

Dirty Bertie

"And in that round, Bertie, you answered no questions and scored no points!" said Donna.

Bertie took a bow. Eugene clapped.

"Yes, very funny," glowered Nick. "A fat lot of use you're going to be."

Dirty Bertie

After school, Bertie dropped in to see his gran. He told her all about the Junior Quiz Challenge and Miss Boot picking him for the team.

"That's wonderful, Bertie!" said Gran.

"No, it's terrible," said Bertie. "I'm rubbish at quizzes and Miss Boot expects us to win."

"Well, maybe you will," said Gran.

"We won't!" Bertie moaned. "We come last every year!"

Gran sighed. "Tell you what," she said, "why don't we call in at the library and find some books to help you."

Bertie couldn't see how books were going to help, but he didn't have any better ideas.

Dirty Bertie

At the library Gran took him upstairs
to the Children's Section.

"So what kind of things do you like?"
she asked.

Bertie shrugged. "Loads of things,"
he said. "Worms, slugs, maggots,
stink-bombs…"

"Hmm," said Gran. "Somehow I doubt
stink-bombs are going to help."

Dirty Bertie

Bertie looked along the shelves —
there was no way he could read this
many books. He might as well face it —
the quiz was going to be one big
disaster. They would end up losing by a
zillion points and Miss Boot would blame
him as usual. He trawled through the
books gloomily. *Ancient Kings and Queens,*
Fun with Fossils, My First Book of
Flowers… Wait a minute, what was this?

"Gran!" called Bertie. "Can I get this
one out?"

"Of course!"
said Gran.
"What is it?"

Bertie held
up the cover
so she could
read it.

CHAPTER 3

For the next two weeks, the quiz team
met to practise every lunchtime. Things
did not improve. Nick grumbled that he
was leading a team of idiots, even though
Donna and Eugene were quite good.
Sadly the same could not be said of
Bertie. The one time he got an answer
right, he ran round the room yelling with

Dirty Bertie

his T-shirt over his head.

All too soon, the day of the Junior Quiz Challenge arrived. Pudsley had been drawn to face last year's finalists, Swotter House. As the coach pulled into the drive, Bertie stared up at the ancient-looking school. Miss Topping, one of the teachers, was waiting to meet them at the door.

"Miss Boot, welcome!" she beamed. "And this must be your quiz team!"

"Yes," said Miss Boot. "This is Nicholas, Donna, Eugene and ... don't do that please, Bertie."

Bertie removed a finger that had crept up his nose. He wiped it on his jumper to show he hadn't forgotten his manners.

"Well," said Miss Topping brightly,

Dirty Bertie

"I'm sure they're cleverer than they look.
May I introduce our team? This is Giles,
Miles, Tara and Harriet. They are so
looking forward to beating … I mean
meeting you."

The Swotter House team shook
hands solemnly. They wore spotless
purple blazers and neatly knotted ties.
Bertie thought they looked like they all
belonged to the same family – the
Frankenstein family.

Dirty Bertie

At two o'clock people began to file into the hall for the start of the quiz. The two teams were seated opposite each other on the stage. The Swotter House team sat up straight. The Pudsley team fidgeted nervously. Miss Boot was in the front row next to Miss Skinner. The hall was filling up with supporters from both schools. Bertie wondered if he should make a run for it now. Know-All Nick leaned over to give his team talk.

"Remember," he whispered. "I'm captain, so let me handle the questions."

"Yeah, but what if you don't know the answers?" said Bertie.

Nick rolled his eyes. "Trust me, I know what I'm doing," he said.

Dirty Bertie

Donna and Eugene exchanged
worried looks. But it was too late to
argue now, Miss Topping was taking her
seat and the quiz was about to start. The
hall lights dimmed. The audience chatter
died down. Miss Topping began by
explaining the rules.

Dirty Bertie

"The first team to buzz may answer," she said. "If you get it wrong, the question passes to the other team."

Both teams nodded. The Junior Quiz Challenge began.

"What do the letters MP stand for?" said Miss Topping.

Dirty Bertie

BUZZ!

"More pudding!" shouted Nick.

"No, I'll pass it over," said Miss Topping.

"Member of Parliament," answered Giles.

"Correct! Who invented the telephone?"

BUZZ! Nick was first again.

"Um…" he said, going red. "Er … it was…"

"Time's up," said Miss Topping. "Swotter House?"

"Alexander Graham Bell," answered Giles.

"Correct!"

CHAPTER 4

The questions went on – and on.
By round three Pudsley were trailing
miserably by 18 points to one. Nick had
answered nineteen questions, and got
eighteen of them wrong.

"What are you doing?" moaned
Donna, when they stopped for a
drinks break.

Dirty Bertie

"We have to buzz first or we'll lose!" said Nick.

"We *are* losing," said Bertie.

"What's the good of buzzing first if you don't know the answer?" complained Eugene.

"It's not my fault!" grumbled Nick. "The questions are too hard!"

"Well, if you carry on like this they're going to batter us," said Bertie.

"Yes, and so will Miss Boot," said Eugene.

They glanced over at their class teacher whose face was like thunder.

"Let me or Eugene answer for a change," said Donna.

"What about me?" asked Bertie.

"Er, well, you too," said Donna. "But only if you're sure you know the answer."

Dirty Bertie

Round four got under way. It was about books.

"Who wrote *The BFG*?"

BUZZ!

Donna got there first.

"Roald Dahl," she answered.

"Correct!"

"Can you name the Famous Five?"

BUZZ!

The scoreboard ticked over. Three rounds later, Swotter House were not looking quite so smug. Thanks to Donna and Eugene, Pudsley had closed the gap to just three points at 34 points to 31. Bertie had still not spoken a word, except to ask if he could go to the toilet. Now everything depended on the final round. The teams leaned forward.

Dirty Bertie

"Our final round is about the human body," said Miss Topping.

Bertie suddenly sat up, paying attention. This was more like it. He'd been reading *Why are Bogeys Green?*, which had a lot to say about the human body.

"What is saliva?" asked Miss Topping.

BUZZ!

"A disease?" asked Giles.

"No, I'm afraid not."

"I know!" shouted Bertie. He buzzed. "Spit!"

"Correct," said Miss Topping. "Which part of the body has half a million sweat glands?"

BUZZ!

"YOUR FEET!" yelled Bertie.

"Correct. What do you produce more of when you're scared?"

Dirty Bertie

BUZZ!

"EARWAX!" cried Bertie.

His teammates stared at him. Surely this had to be wrong?

"Correct!" said Miss Topping. "What—"

BEEP! BEEP! BEEP! The timer interrupted, bringing the quiz to an end. The scores were level at 34 points each. Miss Topping announced the contest would be decided by a tiebreak question.

"Whoever answers correctly is the winner," she said, glaring at the Swotter House team.

The teams sat on the edge of their seats, their fingers poised to buzz. Miss Boot chewed her fingernails.

Dirty Bertie

"What did the Romans use as toothpaste?" asked Miss Topping.

The hall fell deadly silent. Seven faces looked blank. Bertie shut his eyes, trying to remember. Toothpaste, what did the Romans use as toothpaste – hadn't he read this somewhere? It was something to do with squirrels or hamsters or…

BUZZ!

"Was it yoghurt?" asked Harriet.

"No. Pudsley, can you answer?"

Everyone turned to Bertie. He opened his eyes.

"MOUSE BRAINS!" he cried.

"EWWW!" groaned the audience. Miss Boot sunk her head in her hands. Trust Bertie to ruin everything.

Dirty Bertie

Miss Topping sighed deeply. "Correct," she said. "Pudsley are the winners."

A deafening cheer shook the hall. Know-All Nick was speechless. Miss Boot and Miss Skinner hugged and danced round the room. For the first time ever, Pudsley had won a quiz contest, and Bertie, of all people, had answered the winning question. He ran round the stage yelling, until he was carried off by his cheering teammates.

Dirty Bertie

"Well, we did it," said Eugene, as they finally left the hall.

"Yes," said Bertie. "Thank goodness it's all over."

"Until next time," said Miss Boot.

Bertie stared at her. "N-next time?"

"Of course," said Miss Boot. "That was just the first round. There's six more before you reach the final!" She thumped him hard on the back. "And we are all counting on you, Bertie!"

Out now!